REALLY
PUZZLED

THE PUZZLED MYSTERY ADVENTURE
SERIES: BOOK 2

P.J. Nichols

Paperback ISBN 978-4-910091-04-4
Hardcover ISBN 978-4-910091-06-8
Audiobook ISBN 978-4-910091-05-1

pjnichols.com

Cover design by Thomas Paehler

For my mom and dad,
You are both rock stars.

CHAPTER 1

"Haven't you ever paddled a canoe before?" Nicola asked playfully, amused by the fact that Peter couldn't get their canoe to do anything other than constantly go in a big circle.

"Gimme a break!" Peter replied while laughing at himself. "Don't tell me that you now expect your boyfriend to be good at sports, too?"

* * *

Nicola had been allowed to join Peter's family for their annual summer camping trip at Starlight Lake National Park. She had begged her mom for months to let her go. She used the fact that she was now fifteen and about to enter high school as her main bargaining chip. Plus she played the "and you've known Peter's dad since you were six card." Clearville was a pretty small town. Her mom had attended the same schools as Peter's dad for thirteen years, and they were even in the same class a number of times.

Peter's older brother Bradley had decided not

to join the annual trip this year. He was signed up to compete in the big district triathlon at the end of September, and he had told his parents he wanted to stay home and train for it. But Peter knew the truth: Having the house to himself was what Bradley was really after. Bradley was a partier. And since the family camping trip was booked for the last week of summer break, Peter had no doubt that Bradley would invite everyone he knew over for a huge bash. He was actually so worried about it that he had removed all of his puzzles and games from his room, and locked them away safely in the attic, out of sight of Bradley's friends.

Since Bradley had talked his way out of going on the trip, the six-seater family van had enough space for one more. So Peter's parents had decided to also let Sophia, his twelve-year-old sister, invite a friend along. Of course she chose Anita, her best friend for as long as everyone could remember. And Anita's home was only three houses down the road, so both sets of parents were friends as well.

* * *

"Wait, I think I just figured it out!" Peter proudly announced as he tried desperately to aim their boat in a straight line for the first time.

"No you didn't!" Nicola answered, laughing so hard that she made a loud snorting sound. "Now we're going sideways!"

It was hard for Peter to believe that he and Nicola had been dating for two years now. For the first few months, he constantly worried that someone bigger, stronger, and cooler would show up and sweep her off her feet. Nicola was incredibly attractive, but luckily for Peter, she was completely disinterested in the strong and handsome jock type. Whenever a guy approached her and asked for a date, she simply said, "Already got a boyfriend." And that was that.

Peter decided to give up on his feeble attempt at looking macho while paddling, and handed Nicola the other oar. He intentionally passed it to her in a way that splashed her with as much water as possible. Nicola responded by rocking the boat to one side so quickly that Peter almost fell overboard.

After they both became tired and sore from maneuvering their canoe around the lake, they slowly started to make their way back to the shore. But instead of taking in the amazing view, Peter and Nicola were pondering what to do for Zoltan's weekly puzzle.

Since taking over as Zoltan's puzzle-maker two years ago, the weekly routine had remained the same for Peter. Zoltan was to be provided with one interesting, challenging, and creative puzzle per week. The weekly puzzle needed to be completely ready by eight o'clock on Sunday morning, regardless of the season or the weather.

Nicola had, of course, offered to help Peter with this immense task, whether that meant coming up with ideas or setting up things.

They'd been doing these for so long now that they were finding it harder and harder to always come up with new and original ideas.

"Why don't we just reuse some old stuff?" Nicola suggested. "I mean, not totally, just partially."

"We better not," Peter replied quickly. "You remember what happened that time when we both had the flu."

* * *

Peter was referring to the very scary event from a year and a half ago, in the third week of January. Both he and Nicola had caught the flu, so neither were able to do anything to prepare Zoltan's weekly challenge. But they knew if they prepared nothing, that Zoltan might create some type of storm or other catastrophe. They were both so miserably sick that all they could do was quickly combine together parts of previous challenges, and hope it would be good enough. They were wrong. Very wrong.

Zoltan always arrived to do his puzzle at eight o'clock on Sunday morning. On that particular Sunday, at exactly 8:22, a horrendous hailstorm hammered down on the town. It was relentless. It shattered and cracked windows of homes, cars, and stores, and sent people running like mad for safety. It was Zoltan's way of telling Peter and Nicola to never try something like that again.

* * *

"But we are seriously out of ideas," Nicola said. "I mean, last week, it took us a whole day just to think of where to start."

As much as he hated to admit it, Nicola was right. These days, they were scraping the bottom of the barrel when it came to creativity.

"But it's only Wednesday," Peter replied. "We've still got a few more days. C'mon, let's worry about that later."

They paddled the final ten minutes or so back to shore in silence. They weren't angry or upset at each other, they were just trying to brainstorm ideas for Zoltan's next puzzle.

As they were pulling the canoe back up on the beach, Peter stopped and snapped his fingers. "Got one!" he said excitedly.

As he prepared to launch into an explanation of his ingenious idea, a cold wind started to pick up. They wanted to be back inside before the weather turned ugly, so they quickly finished securing the canoe, and headed for the shelter of the cabin.

But the wind rapidly increased in intensity and as the sky darkened, it suddenly got a lot colder.

"What's going on?" Nicola asked while pulling her hood up over her head to block the wind.

"I don't know," Peter replied.

Before he could say another word, they both watched a huge tornado touch down in the middle of the lake.

"Look!" Nicola yelled. "C'mon, we've gotta get back to the cabin!"

They ran back to the rental cabin, fighting hard to keep their balance. Once safely inside, they watched in amazement from the window. The tornado was enormous. It was fierce. They pleaded for it to stay far from the shore, as it would certainly tear apart their flimsy log cabin if it came too close. Thankfully, it remained over the lake.

Two long and agonizing minutes later, the tornado magically vanished, and the peaceful weather returned.

While everyone else breathed a sigh of relief, Peter and Nicola looked at each other in shock. Peter's stomach started churning, just like it did every time he had to give speeches at school.

"Zoltan knows he has to wait until Sunday for his puzzle," he whispered in Nicola's ear. "What's he doing? Why is he so angry?"

Too many questions and no quick or easy way to find the answers. Well, so much for the relaxing escape from city life...

CHAPTER 2

They arrived back home from their camping trip late Friday afternoon. Peter's dad always booked the cabin from Sunday through Friday, as the weekend rental fee was outrageous.

They spent about thirty minutes unpacking and putting everything where it belonged. Peter's mom was a neat freak, so things always had to be put away as fast as humanly possible. Once they were done, Peter and Nicola went upstairs to his room.

"Okay," he said with an anxious look on his face. "First, we need to contact Zoltan so we can ask him why on Earth he did that."

After the flu incident, Peter and Zoltan had arranged a way to contact each other whenever necessary. If Zoltan wanted to get in touch, he would tape a leaf on the outside of Peter's bedroom window. And if Peter wanted to call Zoltan, he would turn on a light which he had installed in the chimney on the roof. (Peter had told his mom he was putting up Christmas lights, and then secretly installed a bright light inside the chimney.) When turned on, no one could see it unless they were above the house. Peter had only used it twice, and both times he felt like he was calling a superhero to come and save the day. It was very simple to turn on: The cord from the light in the chimney came to just outside Peter's window. All he had to do was attach it to an extension cord (which he kept hidden in his closet) and plug it in.

And regardless of whom called whom, the meeting place and time were both fixed: The bottom of Silverhead Mountain, at nine in the morning, on the nearest Saturday.

They plugged in the light and went back downstairs.

"Nicola, you're welcome to stay for dinner if you want," Peter's mom said. "It's nothing fancy, just spaghetti."

"Thank you for the offer," she replied politely. "But I think I better head home. My parents only agreed to let me go camping if I promised to do a huge pile of chores as soon as I got home."

* * *

Later that night, Peter puttered around in his room well after he should have been asleep. He always needed to reason everything out. He hated unanswered *whys*, and right now there were way, way too many of them.

He unplugged the chimney light, turned off the lights in his room, and picked up his glow-in-the-dark dice, a present he received from Nicola last Christmas. Wow, did that girl ever know how to get to Peter's heart! He tossed the dice back and forth between his hands for a while, and the movement of the colors helped Peter to finally doze off a few minutes past midnight.

CHAPTER 3

The next morning, Saturday, Peter cycled up
Nicola's driveway at exactly 8:40. Another one of
Peter's quirks was his obsession with preciseness.
Be there by 8:45 meant I'll be there way before
8:45, because I want to make absolutely sure that
there is no possibility of being even a second late.

Nicola knew Peter's character well by now, and
was already waiting for him on the front steps.
They could easily cycle out to Silverhead
Mountain in less than fifteen minutes, which
would leave them some time to spare while
waiting for Zoltan.

Peter still hadn't decided exactly what to say
to Zoltan. He knew he shouldn't appear too angry.
They were dealing with a supernatural being
with unbelievably destructive powers, right? But
at the same time, Peter was still upset and
wanted Zoltan to know that there were better and
far less dangerous ways to get their attention.

Zoltan showed up at exactly nine o'clock,

literally coming out of nowhere. He always just *appeared* for their meetings. He never walked or rode in, or arrived by any means that would make him seem somewhat human.

And as always, Zoltan waited for Peter and Nicola to approach first. Peter quickly stormed over, as he was extremely anxious to know what was going on.

"What was with that tornado at the lake on Wednesday?" he asked very loudly and directly.

"Yeah," Nicola quickly followed, also unable to contain her frustration. "You could have hurt someone!"

Zoltan was silent. And since his face was hidden by his hood, neither Peter nor Nicola could gauge his reaction.

"C'mon!" Peter asked again loudly. "What's going on?!"

"This is quite perplexing," Zoltan replied. "I did not make a tornado, at a lake, on Wednesday. I have not made any tornados, anywhere, for ages."

"Gimme a break!" Peter said back sharply. "It was NOT a natural one."

"Whether or not it was natural, I can't say," Zoltan answered. "But what I can tell you for sure is that *I* did not cause it."

A long silence ensued. Someone was lying. Or maybe they weren't. Or, quite possibly, they were all just really confused. Peter shuffled around, impatiently waiting for Zoltan's next comment. He needed a feasible explanation, and he wanted it now.

Zoltan turned around to walk away.

"Where do you think you're going?!" Nicola yelled at him.

Zoltan stopped, but he didn't turn around to face them. "You asked me a question, and I answered it," he said coldly. "I have no idea what caused that tornado."

Peter looked at Nicola, shrugged his shoulders, and started heading toward his bike. There was no point in arguing about something that all three of them didn't understand.

Just as he was about to sit down on the bike seat, someone kicked or jerked his bike hard. Peter lost his balance, and both he and his bike toppled over sideways. He twisted around to scold Nicola for her untimely and immature little prank.

"Nik, what are you...?" he said angrily.

But Nicola was at least four or five meters away. She clearly hadn't done anything.

Before he could say anything, the ground started shaking violently. An earthquake?! Peter couldn't believe his eyes. He turned in the direction he had last seen Zoltan to scream at him. But Zoltan was already facing them, with his hands in his pockets, and his hood off for the first time ever. Peter and Nicola were startled by

Zoltan's face: Not because he looked like a monster or zombie, but by the fact that he looked so human. And the expression on Zoltan's face showed that he was just as confused as they were about the earthquake.

Since they were outside, they were relatively safe. It wasn't like something would fall from above and injure them. All they had to do was wait it out. But when a person panics, especially a nervous kid like Peter, logic doesn't always prevail. Peter darted around aimlessly, looking up in fear at the shaking tree branches. It was as if he were riding a surfboard while dancing the tango. Even Zoltan, who never showed any emotion, cracked a smile while watching Peter's performance.

When the shaking finally stopped, Zoltan walked over to Nicola and Peter. "Well, now you know I wasn't lying," he said very matter-of-factly.

"But hold on a sec," Peter said while trying to catch his breath, his heart still beating insanely fast. "If it wasn't you, then who? Or what? There are no fault lines around here. It's completely impossible for earthquakes to happen in this region. That earthquake was NOT natural."

"Yeah, he's right," Nicola added. "Zoltan, what's going on?"

Zoltan pulled his hood back over his head, and turned to walk away again.

When he was a few meters away from them, he twisted his head back to say something. "As you know," he said seriously, "I am the only weather god assigned to Earth. But it would appear, for a reason I don't know, that we have company. I'll look into it. Meet me back here tomorrow. And you can forget about my weekly challenge. There is no longer any time for games."

CHAPTER 4

Peter's house had been completely undamaged by the earthquake. His family, and all of the neighbors, hadn't even noticed it. If it had been a natural earthquake, it would definitely have been felt throughout the whole town. So that just reinforced Peter's theory that someone had both caused it and focused it on only the area they were in at the time. But the notion that there might be another weather god on Earth made Peter nauseous.

* * *

Unfortunately, Peter had the bad habit of worrying himself sick. He hated his overly active mind, which had to play out every possible negative outcome, as if one of them was guaranteed to happen. Back when he was eight, his parents went to Europe for five days, on a trip they had won from a cereal box sweepstakes competition. While they were gone, Peter's grandparents walked him to the school bus every morning. While waiting for the bus, he'd say, "I feel like I'm gonna barf." Peter was paranoid that an engine failure was going to cause the plane to crash somewhere over the Atlantic Ocean. His grandparents took him home and allowed him to miss school for the day. Shortly after arriving home, he would throw up, sometimes more than once. When you're a worrier, you can never, ever turn it off.

* * *

Peter tossed and turned all night. His stomach was in such a knot the next morning that he could barely even manage a few spoons of cereal. But breakfast or no breakfast, Peter needed to get to Silverhead Mountain again. Hopefully, Zoltan would have some information for them, as there was no way he could possibly get back to normal life until he knew more.

* * *

Zoltan was already waiting for them when they arrived, and he uncharacteristically waved when he saw them coming.

"Since when did he develop a personality?" Peter whispered to Nicola. "He must be even more scared than we are."

"Good to see you both again," Zoltan said as Peter and Nicola sat down. "I managed to find out a few things yesterday."

"A *few* things?" Peter asked. "What do you mean?"

"I don't want to bore you with a long lecture on the history and bloodlines of weather gods," Zoltan began. "But without a brief one, none of this will make any sense. I'll try to keep it as short as I can.

"As you already know, I was sent to Earth about twenty-eight years ago, as a punishment of sorts. You remember why the lead weather gods sent me here, right? Because I tried to cheat my way into being assigned to a small and easy planet. Well, I've always assumed that I was the only weather god to ever receive any type of punishment. There are no courts or judges or prisons where I'm from, and I'd never heard any stories about weather gods causing even the slightest trouble. But was I ever wrong.

"It would appear that I have an older brother. Much older. And I only learned about his existence last night. You know the fairy tale about the girl with the evil stepsisters? I suppose you could say I have an evil brother. And it's my brother, in fact, that's been causing the weather problems here recently."

"Your brother?" Peter said, dumbfounded. "But why would he come to Earth? And why would he start messing with the weather here? It makes zero sense."

"It didn't make any sense to me either," Zoltan replied. "Well, until last night. As outrageous as this may sound, my brother, whose name is

Xavier by the way, is here to get revenge."

"Revenge?" Nicola asked. "On whom? For what?"

"On me," Zoltan answered. "I'll fill you in on the rest later, I promise. I must go now. I need to find out as much as I can about Xavier."

Peter and Nicola watched as Zoltan started walking away very quickly.

"Meet me here again on Wednesday morning!" he yelled back at them.

"But school starts this week," Peter said back. "Can't we wait until next weekend?"

Zoltan stopped walking and turned around to face them. "No, we can't wait that long," he said very sternly. "Just skip school on Wednesday. See you then."

CHAPTER 5

Peter had missed a few days of school here and there whenever he was sick, but he had never intentionally played hooky. He had wanted to do so on many occasions, but was terrified of the possible consequences. More specifically, he feared the wrath that would come down from his mother. She had absolutely no patience for kids with a slack attitude. He'd seen Bradley punished for skipping school more times than he could count.

Peter had thought up a very believable lie to get himself and Nicola out of school for the day. It was extremely simple. And, well, simple is always best, right?

On Wednesday morning, he left for school a couple of minutes earlier than usual and rode directly to Nicola's house. Her parents were both nurses, and were currently working the 6 a.m. to 4 p.m. shift, so that meant Nicola would be the only one home.

The *trick* to getting them out of school was going to be implemented by Nicola. She was going to make two calls to the school: one posing as Peter's mom, and one posing as her own mother. She'd wait at least fifteen minutes between calls, to reduce the chance of arousing any suspicion. But they actually weren't too worried about the phone calls raising any red flags. Their high school's one and only receptionist, Miss Perkins, apparently had a reputation for always being buried in fashion magazines. (That was something Bradley had mentioned quite a few times.) The likelihood of her noticing that the two calls had come from the same person or even the same number was virtually zero, especially if Nicola used a deeper voice for one of the calls.

As expected, all went smoothly. Nicola was going to miss the morning, and possibly the whole day, to get a filling at the dentist. And Peter had a nasty case of diarrhea, so he couldn't possibly make it to school today. As long as they both returned to school on Thursday and stuck to their stories, it was highly unlikely that anyone from the school would phone to confirm. Well, unless someone spotted them outside somewhere today...

Thankfully, small towns have plenty of side streets, paths, and parks. They could easily navigate their way to Silverhead Mountain using a route that would put them at very little risk of being seen.

* * *

They got there a couple of minutes later than expected, and Zoltan was already waiting as promised. He waved again today when he saw them approaching, and this time he was holding a bag with some cookies and juice boxes he'd just bought at a convenience store.

After exchanging a few quick pleasantries and happily getting started on their snacks, they all sat down at one of the picnic tables.

"We are going to be here for a while today," Zoltan began. "What's going on is far, far worse than I originally thought.

"I suppose I should start by explaining everything I just learned about my long-lost brother. When he was very young, way before I was even born, people realized his weather altering skills were developing faster than anyone in history. By the age of eight, he was already more powerful than most of the adults. The young Xavier loved all of the attention. People came from far and wide to catch a glimpse of this prodigy. They wanted to see, with their own two eyes, the kid who was destined to become the greatest weather god ever.

"And then when Xavier was fourteen, I was born. You'd think that he would've been happy to get a sibling after being an only child for so long, but his reaction was the complete opposite. He despised that his parents' time was now split between him and a screaming baby. He just couldn't tolerate the fact that he was no longer the center of his parents' world.

"His attitude turned full circle, and he started to rebel. He wouldn't listen to anyone and began doing whatever he wanted. When my parents tried to punish him for any type of inexcusable behavior, he rebelled even more. Then one day, he did the unthinkable; he snuck out after dark and unleashed an enormous storm, centered directly on our home. And since it was the dead of night, no one noticed in time to try to stop him.

"Our house was reduced to rubble, and we were all seriously injured. I was still a baby, but somehow my mom managed to grab me from my crib before the roof collapsed. We were lucky to make it out alive.

"But before Xavier could be caught and punished for his brutal act, he vanished. And no one has heard from him since. Well, until now.

"In his mind, I destroyed his ideal world. Xavier truly hates me. He despises me. And he wants me to suffer. He believes I ruined his world, so now he wants to ruin mine."

"So how do we stop him?" Peter asked.

"We don't," Zoltan replied. "We can't. He is far too powerful. He could, and I'm not joking, wipe out everyone on Earth in a few weeks if he really wanted to. During all those years since he went into hiding, he must have been honing his destructive powers."

"So what do we do?" Peter asked again.

"There is only one thing I can imagine that might work," Zoltan replied. "We have to trick him or fool him. And then finally, trap him."

"Trap him?" asked Nicola. "But how do we trap someone so powerful?"

"Our trap will have to be something he won't see coming," Zoltan said. "We have to create a trap that he'll never suspect is a trap."

"Uh... I'm a little lost," Peter said. "How do we do that?"

"Oh, I haven't thought of *how* to trap him yet," Zoltan replied. "That's what I need you two for!"

CHAPTER 6

Peter was unbelievably paranoid about being caught skipping school. Right now, he really wished he had an invisibility cloak, as that would guarantee him safe passage home. Too bad he didn't live in a world of magic...

They rode home on the same seldomly used streets and paths, stopping at the end of each one to make sure there was no one was around the next corner. And they timed it so they'd arrive home at roughly the same time as any other school day. They had even taken their backpacks with them, filled with schoolbooks, to ensure everything appeared completely normal.

* * *

Only Sophia was home when Peter got back. He casually walked into the kitchen and grabbed some chocolate chip cookies and a glass of milk, just as he would on a typical day after school. Then he carried them to the family room, placed them down on the coffee table, and grabbed the

TV remote. Sophia came and sat down beside him, likely because she was bored and had nothing better to do.

"Guess what happened today?" she said excitedly. "You remember Mr. Phillips, right? You know, the science teacher. When he turned on the overhead projector, the words 'I am a dork' shone up on the screen! Someone, maybe Keith or Tony, had written it on there between classes. It was like, soooo funny! He went crazy!"

Peter was trying to listen to his sister's story, but everything she said was going in one ear and out the other. He kept thinking about whether he was acting normal or not. He didn't want to do anything to tip Sophia off to the fact he'd played hooky.

"That's cool," he replied, not really knowing what else to say. "Mr. Phillips has been a grump, like, forever. I never saw that guy smile."

"Yeah, no kidding," she said. Then she got up and skipped happily out of the room.

Alone again in the family room, Peter felt like he was in some weird and bizarre trance. He looked down at the empty plate and glass on the coffee table, but he couldn't remember taking a bite of a cookie or a sip of milk. But when a chocolaty, milky burp suddenly came out, he realized that he had indeed finished his snack.

* * *

Right after dinner, Peter went up to his room,

locked the door, and sat at his desk. He grabbed a sheet of loose-leaf paper and wrote "How to Trick Xavier" at the top. Peter approached every challenging puzzle the same way: He started by putting all his ideas down on paper. Then he eliminated the bad ones before continuing. This technique helped Peter save tons of time.

CHAPTER 7

A ridiculous dream, which involved dancing babies and giant talking vegetables, startled Peter awake. He had been sleeping face down on his desk for hours, and a small pile of drool had formed on the list he'd spent so much time writing.

Peter checked his wristwatch. It was a quarter past nine. No wonder his neck hurt so much. He pulled a couple of tissues from the box on his desk and wiped the spit off his papers.

The list was so messy and disorganized that 99.999 percent of the population would have no chance of understanding it. First, he had scribbled down every single idea, good or bad, that had popped into his mind. Then when he could come up with no more, the next steps were to eliminate some, link some with circles and lines, and add more detail to the good ones. What he had produced in the end looked like a cross between the brainstorming of Einstein and the doodling of a two-year-old.

Peter knew he wouldn't be able to get back to sleep, so he grabbed a fresh sheet of paper and started on a more organized version of the first list. Once he'd rewritten everything, he leaned back in his chair and smiled. He had managed to come up with a masterful plan to first trick, and then trap, Xavier. It wasn't going to be easy, but if somehow they could pull off everything to perfection, it would work.

Just like two years ago, the innocent people of earth needed to be saved, and Peter was the only person capable of doing it. But why now? It didn't seem fair. He was enjoying life. He had the perfect girlfriend. Everything was just like he had hoped for in his wildest dreams.

Peter thought about what his dad would say when someone started complaining about how hard things were: *Too bad, so sad*. Peter had never understood where his dad got all of the weird expressions. But he kind of felt like he had finally figured out the meaning of this one: *Stop whining and complaining, and get on with it.*

CHAPTER 8

Despite the urgency of getting started on the plan, skipping school again today was not an option. Peter and Nicola had gone undetected yesterday, but another absence would certainly raise some eyebrows. And if they did try and were caught, Peter knew his mom would ground him for at least a week. He wouldn't be allowed to go anywhere other than school. Plus no friends would be allowed to come over. That would end up being counter-productive, as it would mean they wouldn't be able to meet Zoltan on the weekend.

So all he could do was wait. Wait and wait and wait some more, until Saturday morning finally arrived.

* * *

At slightly before nine on Saturday morning, Peter, Nicola, and Zoltan were sitting at a picnic table at Silverhead Mountain again. Peter launched into the explanation of his complicated and confusing plan. He tried to cover everything, leaving out no details at all. Nicola had trouble wrapping her head around a lot of it, and Zoltan had to ask for clarification numerous times.

Just before noon, it seemed as if they were both up to speed on everything. They knew what they had to do, and exactly how they had to do it. It was going to be an extremely challenging and complex process. But if each and every part of the plan could be done to perfection, then a couple of weeks from today, Xavier would be trapped. And once trapped, he could then be banished from Earth forever.

CHAPTER 9

The first part of the ingenious plan would be initiated that very afternoon. But before getting started, they decided to grab a quick sandwich at a small café on the edge of town. Peter had brought a pair of his dad's jeans and a t-shirt for Zoltan to use today, as Zoltan's usual cloak would have attracted way too much attention. Dressed in Peter's dad's clothes, Zoltan managed to blend in just fine.

After lunch, the three of them returned to Silverhead Mountain. What they needed to do first was to get Xavier's attention. They climbed as far up the mountain as they could, until it would have been dangerous to go any further. It was exhausting, but they were able to get within about a hundred meters of the peak.

"This should be high enough," Peter said, huffing and puffing. Although Peter was reasonably good at most of the sports he did in gym class, climbing a steep mountain was another story altogether. "Alright, Zoltan, you know what to do."

Zoltan's face hardened, and he raised his hands in the air. He started chanting something, which Peter knew was his way of commanding the weather. Zoltan easily created a massive storm, which pounded hard against the lower half of the mountain.

"Xavier will definitely see this!" Peter yelled at Nicola through the noise. "I mean, how could he not?"

Zoltan gradually increased the ferocity of the storm. Within less than two minutes, it was so huge that making it any bigger would start to uproot small trees or possibly even initiate a landslide.

"Still no sign of Xavier..." Peter said. "Now what?"

Zoltan, looking somewhat burnt out from his efforts, decided to add some fireworks to the mix. He made loud claps of thunder and bolt after bolt of lightning.

"He's gotta notice soon," Nicola said. "Why isn't he here yet?"

Zoltan's arms were now trembling. Clearly this was taking a huge toll on him. Peter figured that Zoltan would be incapable of maintaining this huge storm much longer.

And then, in an instant, the storm completely vanished.

"Are you okay?" Peter yelled while spinning around to look at Zoltan. He figured that Zoltan had overexerted himself and passed out. But Zoltan was just fine, and by the bewildered look on his face, it was obvious that he was just as confused as they were.

Realizing how strange he looked with his arms high up in the air, Zoltan lowered them and put his hands in his pockets. "This is far worse than I feared," he said. "Xavier's powers are beyond what I could have imagined. Stopping another weather god's storm, or even just reducing its intensity, is extremely difficult. Nearly impossible, actually. He made mine vanish instantaneously. I've never heard of anyone capable of doing that."

"Guys, don't worry about that yet," Nicola said supportively. "I mean, we came here to get his attention, right? And we just did that. Now all we have to do is wait and see when he—"

But before she could finish her sentence, the infamous Xavier appeared behind them. Aside from his golden cloak and somewhat messy hair, he was the spitting image of Zoltan. If it wasn't for the fourteen-year age gap, you'd have thought they were twins.

"You're even weaker than I thought!" Xavier said loudly. "I can't believe they sent you to Earth. You're not capable of controlling the weather here!"

As they had planned, Zoltan began taunting

his evil brother. "Gimme a break," he said. "I could've made that storm a hundred, or even a thousand times more powerful if I had wanted to."

"Ha!" Xavier laughed back. "I'd love to see that!"

"Anyway," Zoltan said sharply. "I know why you're here. You came to get revenge, right? Revenge because you think I destroyed your ideal world so many, many years ago. Well, let's just cut to the chase. I want you gone. Now."

"Oh, I see," Xavier replied. "The *good* son, the one mom and dad love the most, wants his bad brother to disappear. You just can't stand to see—"

"Xavier," Zoltan said, interrupting his brother. "This isn't about who's good or who's bad. Earth is *my* planet to manage. I was assigned here by the lead weather gods. And although you may seriously doubt this, I am completely capable of carrying out my duties."

Xavier let out a huge roar. "Stop! Please!" he said while laughing. "I'm going to pee my pants."

"What makes you think you are so special?" Zoltan continued, trying to rile his brother up even more.

"You stupid and naïve brat!" Xavier screamed. He put his palms and fingertips together and raised them up to the sky.

A powerful bolt of lightning came down

directly on Zoltan's head, causing him to jerk and quiver, and then fall over sideways. Peter and Nicola ran over, but Zoltan was unconscious.

"Don't worry, he'll be fine in a couple of weeks," Xavier said. "I want to watch him suffer, not die."

As much as he felt like yelling at Xavier, Peter knew he had to keep his mouth shut. Zoltan could recover from a lightning blast, but he and Nicola certainly could not.

"Nik," Peter whispered. "Don't look at Xavier. Just put your hand on Zoltan's head and act really worried. Make yourself cry or something."

She did as Peter had instructed, and less than thirty seconds later, tears were streaming down her cheeks. Peter, though a poorly skilled actor, did his best to squeeze out a few tears as well.

"You stupid kids," Xavier said while shaking his head. "Why do you care about my brother? He's weak! He's useless! He's a complete joke! *I* am the real thing!"

Despite being terrified beyond belief, Peter and Nicola stuck to the original plan. They needed Xavier to think they loved Zoltan as if he were family. This crucial point would become essential later on.

"Look at me!" Xavier yelled. "You heard me, LOOK!!"

They turned to face him, their cheeks red and wet from crying. "Please leave Zoltan alone," Peter begged. "Please. He helps people. He would

35

never, ever hurt anyone."

"I know that," Xavier barked back. "He's not powerful enough to hurt anyone. Anyway, I have better things to do than sit around here and listen to you crybabies."

Xavier created a dust storm, and as more and more dust began swirling, Peter and Nicola couldn't see him clearly anymore. Once the dust storm had dissipated, Xavier was gone.

"How'd I do?" Zoltan asked while sitting up. "He thought I was out cold, didn't he?"

"You were perfect!" Nicola replied, slapping him lightly on the shoulder. "But that lightning bolt must have hurt."

"Not at all," he said. "Look."

Zoltan showed them the thin and nearly invisible wire he had rigged up, which went from the tip of his cloak's hood to the ground behind him.

"You know how lightning works," he said. "It always takes the easiest path. And a wire is a much better conductor than a person's body. Xavier's lightning bolt didn't touch me at all. It only went through the wire."

"Man, science is cool," Peter said with a smile.

CHAPTER 10

The next part of the plan was linked to what had happened at Silverhead Mountain yesterday. What they needed to do next, in a nutshell, was to make Xavier feel jealous. And not just a little jealous, but so jealous that it would consume him.

They decided to change up their meeting spot today, as they figured that Xavier may come looking for them at Silverhead Mountain.

"I don't get it," Nicola said to Peter, as they rode toward Meeks Park to meet up with Zoltan. "If we rattle him too much, he might go berserk and unleash a huge hurricane or something."

"Yeah, I suppose he could," Peter replied. "We are taking a risk. But my gut tells me he won't. Let's hope my gut is right on this one."

* * *

Zoltan was waiting for them at a picnic table by the river. These days, he seemed more like an *odd-ball uncle* than a supernatural being. And his people skills were getting much better too.

"Yo," Zoltan said while waving them over.

Both Peter and Nicola held back their laughter, not wanting Zoltan to know how ridiculous he sounded when trying to talk like a teenager.

"No aftereffects from that lightning bolt yesterday?" Peter asked as he and Nicola sat down. "Are you sure none of that lightning went through you?"

"I'm totally fine, dudes," Zoltan replied, sounding even more ridiculous than before.

"Quite the group you've got here!" a raspy voice said from behind them.

They all turned to see Mr. Winchester slowly walking their way. He looked way younger than he had two years ago, when he was on the brink of death from pushing himself too hard while training Peter's team. But since he no longer had any responsibilities, he was now able to maintain a fairly healthy lifestyle. He occupied most of his free time playing chess with his newfound friends at the community center. And when he couldn't find anyone to play against, he buried his head into a crossword or Sudoku puzzle.

"Leonardo, you look great," Zoltan said while standing up to shake his former entertainer's hand.

"I figure I got a few good years left in me still," Mr. Winchester replied with a big smile. "And by the sound of what's going on, you'll need all the help you can get."

There was, of course, a reason behind why Mr. Winchester had shown up today. Peter had phoned him last night, and they spent close to an hour discussing what had happened already and what was being planned next. Despite his age, Mr. Winchester felt he could still provide some good suggestions and guidance. And when he offered to help, Peter was ecstatic.

After giving Zoltan and Mr. Winchester a chance to catch up and reminisce about the past for a while, Peter figured it was time to get down to business. "Here's what we do next," he said. "Xavier thinks he almost killed Zoltan yesterday. We are going to use that to our advantage. We are going to milk it for all it's worth."

"Milk it?" Zoltan asked. He knew what milk was, but clearly didn't understand all the colloquial expressions or slang yet.

"Anyway," Peter continued quickly, not wanting to waste time explaining what *milk it* actually meant. "Here's the plan: Mr. Winchester, you will fake a heart attack, or something like that, and get yourself hospitalized."

"Hospitalized?" Mr. Winchester replied. "Why would I—"

"Let me explain," Peter said before the old man had a chance to finish his sentence. He hadn't meant to be rude; he just wanted everyone to listen to the whole explanation and save any questions for the end. "What we need is a bed in a hospital room. Once you've been admitted, Zoltan will show up as a visitor. When no one is watching, you'll quickly swap clothes and he'll replace you in the bed. And then he'll lie there and look like he's on the verge of death."

"Peter," Mr. Winchester said with curiosity. "Why would we want to hospitalize Zoltan? How would that do anything other than just make Xavier smile?"

"Because," Peter continued, "I am going to have a least a hundred people come to visit the *almost dead* Zoltan in that hospital room. We know Xavier will be curious about how badly he harmed his brother, right? That means he'll be hanging around somewhere near the hospital. We are going to show him the last thing he wants to see: Tons and tons of people coming to pray for his brother's recovery."

"Yeah, don't you get it?" Nicola added. "When he sees all these teenagers coming to visit his brother, he'll get soooo jealous. Xavier wants to be the center of attention. He'll go insane with jealousy when he sees how much love and respect people have for Zoltan."

"I have more questions about this plan than you could possibly imagine," Mr. Winchester said. "But you have proven yourself countless times before, and I'm sure you know what you're doing. You just tell me when you want me to fake that heart attack."

"Wednesday morning," Peter replied immediately. "I'll need until then to get things set up."

CHAPTER 11

Peter and Nicola came directly back to his house, and were now eating lunch in the family room while looking over the next part of the plan on Peter's master list. The next thing they had to do was going to be really tough, and they knew they couldn't do it without some more assistance. Peter could think of no one better than Neil, one of his closest friends, to help them out.

Peter and Neil had been hanging out a lot since they teamed up to take on Zoltan two years ago. But in the past six months, they only got together a few times. The tall, skinny, and dorky Neil had put on a lot of muscle during Grade 8, plus he changed his hairstyle and fashion choices before starting Grade 9. In doing so, he had managed to become quite a hunk, and droves of girls became interested in him.

After a few relationships that lasted a few weeks each, or in some cases even less, Neil had finally found someone suitable. Claire, a tall girl with long auburn hair and the captain of the girls' volleyball team, had stolen Neil's heart. They were inseparable. When Peter did manage to get together with Neil, it was almost always for a double date. But Peter was truly happy for his friend. Claire seemed to ignore all of Neil's oddities, and they were always laughing and having fun.

Peter and Nicola knocked on Neil's door a little before three o'clock. They had phoned him after lunch, and he told them that he and Claire were watching a DVD at his house. He said they were welcome to drop by anytime in the afternoon.

"Come on in, your majesties," Neil said, bowing deeply to Peter and Nicola. "Your arrival is a true honor."

"Neil, stop that," Claire said from behind him. "You're embarrassing Pete. His face is all red."

Claire was right, on both counts. Even though Peter was only slightly embarrassed, his face and ears were bright pink. Peter had spent years and years wishing he had a complexion that was a little better at hiding his emotions.

Claire ran over and grabbed Nicola's hand. "Nik, you're coming upstairs with me," she said. "I've got some juicy gossip you've gotta hear. And these boys' ears are not privileged to hear this stuff."

Nicola wasn't really one for gossiping, but she needed to be a polite house guest. Plus it would give Peter the chance to explain everything about Zoltan and Xavier to Neil.

* * *

"Pete, this is seriously bad, man," Neil said after listening intently to the information about Zoltan's evil brother and the basic outline of the near impossible task that lay ahead.

"Yeah, it's pretty dire," Peter replied. "But at least we have a ray of hope. If, and only if, we can pull off everything perfectly."

"Well, I'm in," Neil said supportively. "You know you can always count on the Neilster."

Peter thought the silly nickname Neil had concocted for himself had gone out of use a couple years ago, but apparently not. The *Neilster* was still alive and kicking.

Peter then went into more detail about what they'd done so far, and how they were currently working on making Xavier jealous. He also explained how he needed Neil's help to get this next part to succeed.

"Petey, my boy," Neil said at the end of the explanation. "I read you loud and clear."

Nicola had heard an earful about how Steve, the captain of the boys' volleyball team, had a massive crush on Courtney. But apparently Courtney preferred Bob over Steve. But Bob was too dumb to notice all the flirting she was doing. Tons of other names and dating rumors were also thrown into the mix, but Nicola had lost track.

"We'll have to do this again soon!" Claire said as Peter and Nicola were tying up their shoes to get ready to head home. "That was so fun!"

"Yeah, let's," Nicola replied, trying to be nice. But she had heard enough gossip in the last thirty minutes to last her a lifetime.

"So will Neil do it? Is he gonna help?" Nicola asked quietly as they got on their bikes.

"You bet," he replied. "The *Neilster* is in, one hundred percent."

"Awesome!" Nicola said. "But is he really still calling himself that??"

CHAPTER 12

On Wednesday afternoon, everything was set up
as planned. Mr. Winchester had faked severe
chests pains just before noon and had been taken
to the hospital in Stoneburg via ambulance. He
was currently hospitalized for more careful
monitoring and testing.

At three thirty, Zoltan arrived at the hospital
and begged the staff to let him go in and see Mr.
Winchester. He said they had known each other
their whole lives.

While Peter scanned the hallway to make sure
no one was coming, the two men quickly changed
clothes, and Zoltan hopped into the hospital bed.
Mr. Winchester simply snuck down the back
stairwell and walked to a coffee shop down the
road.

As soon as Mr. Winchester was out of sight,
Peter rejoined Neil and Nicola outside the front
doors of the hospital. Just as they had hoped, tons
of kids from their high school started showing up

just before four o'clock, all looking extremely sad and emotional.

Neil and Nicola were in charge of keeping the students lined up in single file, starting a few meters from the doors and running down the sidewalk. Peter was going to take four students up at a time to see Zoltan. Each student would wish Zoltan a speedy recovery, shed a few tears, and be taken back outside and thanked for coming.

"Look how long the line is," Neil whispered in Nicola's ear. "There's at least, like, a hundred people here."

"Yeah, this is perfect," she replied. "It'll take an hour or so for everyone to get in and out. Xavier will surely notice this."

Neil and Nicola made sure the line didn't get in the way of anyone entering or exiting the hospital. They didn't want someone to complain, as a complaint would likely prompt a visit from unhappy hospital personnel.

Peter quickly took group after group up to see Zoltan, using a staircase that couldn't be seen from the front desk. All went smoothly, and about ninety minutes later, he escorted the final four students back to the front doors and thanked them. Zoltan had had 124 visitors in total. They were hoping that Xavier had been watching from somewhere. Peter and his team were counting on it. Actually, they were depending on it.

"How'd it go?" Mr. Winchester asked as he walked up to the flower garden behind the hospital: the place where they had agreed to meet. The old man had finished three cups of coffee and read through every free newspaper at the coffee shop.

"Perfect," Peter replied. "Well, I think it went perfectly."

"But I still don't understand how you convinced over a hundred high school kids to come here and look so devastated," Mr. Winchester said. "Did you bribe them or something?"

"We did better than that," Neil replied, handing Mr. Winchester one of the light green flyers in his hand.

Open Auditions Today!

Stoneburg Memorial Hospital. Starting at 4:00 pm sharp.

Look as sad as you can while lining up and then wishing a speedy recovery to a very sick man. The best 2 performers will be hired for a video we are making, and paid $50 each.

Peter, Neil, Nicola

"You tricksters," Mr. Winchester said while laughing. "That was clever!" After a brief pause, and a little more thinking, he continued, "But tomorrow morning at school, won't people be asking who won? They'll be expecting to hear the winners' names. And then those winners will be owed fifty dollars each. And you'll—"

"No need to worry, Mr. Winchester," Peter said, interrupting the old man. "We'll pick two kids and pay them tomorrow morning. We've got enough cash between the three of us to cover that. Then we'll just say we're still working on the writing part of the video script. As long as they get their money, I doubt they'll care about actually having to do any acting."

Now all they needed to do was get Mr. Winchester back in his hospital bed before six o'clock, when dinner would arrive. No one would ever discover what had just happened.

CHAPTER 13

On Sunday morning, after four nights in the hospital, Mr. Winchester was released with a clean bill of health. The doctors had run numerous tests on him and had been monitoring his vital signs diligently, and decided he was in good enough shape to return home. This was the obvious outcome of course, as the whole *chest pains* thing was completely fake from the start.

But all their efforts would end up being in vain if Xavier saw Zoltan looking fine again too quickly, so they needed to keep up the façade. Mr. Winchester had set up the guest room in his house for Zoltan to use during this *staged* recovery. Zoltan was currently lying in bed there, awaiting the arrival of his evil brother.

* * *

Since today, Monday, was a professional development day for every teacher in town, there was no school. Peter, Nicola, and Neil arrived at Mr. Winchester's home mid-morning. Now all they could do was wait.

* * *

As expected, Xavier did show up, once again in spectacular fashion. In the early afternoon, he came *spinning* down to the front yard of Mr. Winchester's house in a long, narrow tornado. Yes, a tornado. Thankfully, it didn't cause any damage to the house or anything around it.

"Was that really necessary?" Mr. Winchester said strongly. "Don't you think you've shown off your powers enough already?"

Peter froze. "Shut up, Mr. Winchester," he whispered. "You're going to get us all killed."

"Get out of my way, old man," Xavier said, pushing Mr. Winchester hard to the side as he walked up the front steps. "Just tell me which room he's in."

"Follow me, sir," Peter said timidly, leading Xavier down the hallway to the last room on the left.

Xavier marched into the guest room and stood directly over the bed where Zoltan lay. "Aw, my poor brother," he said sarcastically. "Did that little lightning bolt of mine really hurt that much? You've been bed-ridden for almost a week now. C'mon, are you really that weak?"

"Xavier," Peter said nervously from behind. "All your brother does is sleep. The only reason they released him from the hospital is because he can finally breathe on his own. He can't hear what you're saying. And even if he could, he certainly can't reply."

"What's this got to do with you?" Xavier snapped back. "Why do you, and all those kids I saw at the hospital on Wednesday, care so much about my stupid brother?"

Peter was smiling on the inside, but made sure it didn't show on his face. This was exactly what they were hoping for.

"Zoltan is a legend, sir," Peter replied. "Everyone in Clearville, well, not just Clearville, everyone everywhere more or less worships him. Thanks to his powers, the weather is kept under control. No more floods. No more droughts. No more hurricanes. He keeps us safe. He's like, a, a god."

"A what?!" Xavier yelled. "Him? A god? This weak, useless, pathetic pile of garbage?!"

"Sir," Peter replied cautiously, "you saw for yourself yesterday how much everyone loves him. If people ever find out that it was you who put him in this state, they will band together and come after you."

"Ha!" he laughed. "And what could you humans possibly do to me?"

Peter had carefully planned what to say when it got to this point. "You're right," he said. "Humans would have no hope against you. I mean, the reason we love Zoltan so much is because of his amazing powers. Who wouldn't, who couldn't, love such a powerful and amazing being?"

Xavier had heard enough. His face grew even redder, and he furrowed his brow. In his mind, all the love and respect his brother was getting was completely undeserved.

"They should be worshipping me!" he yelled at his brother. "I'm way more powerful than you! You are nothing compared to me! NOTHING!!"

Xavier then turned around and stormed out without looking at anyone. This was good news for Peter and his team, as it meant the seeds of jealousy had been successfully planted.

Once Xavier was gone, they all went back to the guest room to congratulate Zoltan on his performance.

"Me?" Zoltan said after getting high-fives from everyone. "I didn't do anything. I just lay here with my eyes closed. It was Peter who did all the talking."

"Anyway," Peter said happily. "The important thing is that we've got Xavier exactly where we want him."

CHAPTER 14

Peter, Neil, and Nicola spent the next few afternoons gathering at Mr. Winchester's home. This gave them the opportunity to carefully discuss and further plan out the next course of action.

Zoltan, as instructed by Peter, was faking a very slow recovery. He began by waking up on Tuesday, a full ten days after Xavier had tried to fry him with the lightning bolt. Then he started sitting up in bed on Wednesday, and attempted to stand up a few times on Thursday.

Their plan for Friday was to have him make a few attempts at walking. And finally, they'd choose a suitable time on Saturday or Sunday to have him try walking out the front door, down the steps, and to the end of the sidewalk. They knew that as soon as Xavier saw his brother up and moving again, he'd quickly show up.

"Pete," Neil said just as everyone was getting set to head home on Thursday before dinner.

"After Xavier arrives, then what?"

"As crazy as this sounds," Peter replied. "We are going to make Xavier want to take over for Zoltan."

"Take over for Zoltan?" Neil said as his eyes opened wide with surprise. "But he would never help people. He'd probably just flood the whole planet or something."

"Don't be silly," Mr. Winchester said, slowly standing up from his rocking chair. "We are going to make Xavier think that being Earth's weather god is the ultimate honor. We want him to imagine himself being worshipped by people all over the globe."

"Okay, I get that part," Neil replied. "But couldn't he just knock off Zoltan and claim himself as the new weather god for Earth?"

"Yes, he certainly could," Peter said. "But I don't think he *would*. He wants to see Zoltan suffer. Really, really suffer. And that won't happen if Zoltan is dead."

"Hmmm..." Neil replied, still appearing a little confused.

"Stick with me, Neil," Peter said supportively. "It'll all make sense in due time."

CHAPTER 15

The team realized that rushing Zoltan's recovery might cause Xavier to become a little suspicious, so they decided to put off the front yard stroll until late on Sunday afternoon.

"Okay, everyone," Mr. Winchester whispered. "It's show time."

With Neil and Peter supporting his arms, Zoltan slowly shuffled across the front porch, from the door toward the steps. They both continued holding onto Zoltan as he began to make his way slowly down the steps. He was doing his best to make it appear extremely difficult, grimacing in pain with each and every movement.

When they reached the bottom of the steps, Peter let go, and Neil helped Zoltan to the end of the sidewalk.

Then Zoltan turned around to face the house, and loudly announced the line Peter had given him, "Let me see if I can do this on my own. Neil, let go of my arm, but stay close. If I start wobbling too much, grab me before I fall."

Nicola and Peter stood on the front porch. Their job was to act as Zoltan's cheerleaders.

"You can do it!" Nicola yelled with a big smile.

"Yeah, one step at a time!" Peter added. "We know how strong you are!"

Zoltan put on quite a performance. He would take a couple of very awkward and shaky steps, and then pause for a few seconds to catch his breath. He also faced the palm of his hand up to Neil twice, as if to say *stop, don't help me*.

On his twelfth step, just as planned, Zoltan started to fall. Neil promptly grabbed his arm and helped him into an upright position again. About two minutes after this near collapse, Zoltan finally managed to get back to the steps and railing. The instant he touched the railing, Peter and Nicola jumped in celebration.

"Awesome!" Peter said happily. "You're on your way to being the Zoltan of old again!"

"You may be right," Zoltan replied, also smiling. "I think I may finally be on the mend."

"We are so, so happy to hear you say that!" Nicola exclaimed, getting ready for the line she had rehearsed. "The world desperately needs you and your powers back!"

They all sat down on the front steps and chatted happily while soaking up the sunshine. A few minutes later, Mr. Winchester came out with lemonade and cookies for everyone.

"You are a true marvel," Mr. Winchester said. "Are you sure you aren't stronger than that silly brother of yours?"

Peter had planned that line too. He knew it would really aggravate Xavier to hear Zoltan being referred to as his superior.

They all felt the ground start to shake. No doubt another earthquake by Xavier. This guy sure didn't like being number two to anyone.

"Zoltan? Stronger than me?" Xavier yelled from the end of the sidewalk. It startled them all, as no one had noticed him there prior to hearing his voice.

Now it was Mr. Winchester's turn to shine. "My dear Xavier," he said as Xavier approached the stairs. "I'm honored to have you visit my home again." He then bowed as if he were addressing royalty.

"Don't start sucking up to me, old man," Xavier replied coldly.

"Obviously you're here to see your brother's miraculous recovery," Mr. Winchester continued. "Quite something, isn't it? We were worried he would never improve."

"Well, maybe I should've hit him with two lightning bolts instead of one," Xavier laughed.

"If you had done that," Mr. Winchester continued, "then you'd be the most hated person on the planet. Everyone here worships Zoltan.

They've never seen anyone with powers like his...
Well, at least not until now."

Peter jumped in, according to plan. "Xavier
may be a little more powerful than Zoltan," he
said. "But he certainly could never match Zoltan's
intelligence."

"Intelligence?!" Xavier yelled so loudly that the
volume almost pierced their ears. "That's the
most ludicrous thing I've ever heard!"

"Don't doubt your younger brother," Mr.
Winchester said boldly. "You'd be surprised how
clever he is."

"Are you all insane!?" Xavier yelled, even
louder than before. "Zoltan's a moron! He couldn't
find his glasses if they were on his head!"

"But sir," Nicola said on cue, "of course you
don't know this, but Zoltan has been doing
extremely challenging puzzles for years and years.
Mr. Winchester used to make them all, and then
Peter and I took over two years ago. And no
matter how hard we make them, he always
figures them out."

"Yeah," Neil added. "I'd even go as far as
saying Zoltan's a genius."

"I can guarantee you," the red-faced Xavier
said while shaking with anger, "that Zoltan's
mind is nothing, NOTHING, compared to mine!"

Peter smiled on the inside again. Everything
was going as planned.

"Give me one of your stupid riddles or puzzles

to solve," Xavier continued. "I promise you I'll solve it in half the time it took Zoltan!"

"Hold on a second, Peter," Mr. Winchester said, exactly as he was supposed to. "We both know that *creating* puzzles is way harder than simply solving them. If he really wants to prove his intelligence, then he should make a puzzle for Zoltan to do."

"With pleasure," Xavier replied quickly. "But he wouldn't even have a hope."

"In my current condition," Zoltan said, "you're probably right. But I'd be happy to have my friends here do it on my behalf."

"These kids?" Xavier laughed. "Are you telling me you'd put your trust in a bunch of teenagers?"

Now Neil was up to bat. "He certainly would," Neil announced proudly. "Two years back, he created eight incredibly difficult puzzles for us. And we solved them all. Every single one!"

"But what's in this for me?" Xavier asked. "Let's say I make a puzzle or riddle or whatever, and then, just like I expect will happen, you don't solve it. Other than pride, I'd come out of this with nothing. It's a pointless waste of time."

"Then let's put more than just pride on the line," Zoltan said while slowly shuffling toward his older brother. "Here's what I propose. You make a series of difficult challenges for my friends to solve. Let's say, uh... five. Five really difficult ones. If they can't solve all five, then you win, and the following two things will happen: You will replace me as Earth's weather god, in a lavish ceremony that people will come from far and wide to see. And I will become your personal servant, for the rest of my existence."

"Now we're talking!" Xavier replied, almost showing the beginnings of a smile. "My own personal servant... I can already imagine all the things I'd make you do. Oh, but I suppose there's a catch, right? I suppose you're going to say that if they *do* solve all five, that I leave Earth and never come back?"

"Yes, something like that," Mr. Winchester said. "Look, if you don't like these terms, then I suppose you could just kill your brother here and now, and declare yourself as Earth's new weather god... But if you do that, you'll have no big welcome ceremony. And no servant. Plus, everyone on Earth will despise you."

"Hmmm..." Xavier said while nodding his head, clearly weighing the pros and cons of their proposal. "Maybe you caught me on a good day. Fine. I agree to your terms." Then he started chuckling as he prepared to walk away. "But you don't actually think these babies have a chance of solving puzzles created by *my* mind, do you? Zoltan, you must be a lot dumber than I thought."

Zoltan had to bite his tongue. An argument right now would be beneficial to absolutely no one. "And I suggest," he said to Xavier, "that we use the same location I used when I created puzzles for them two years ago: the ancient ruins at Silverhead Mountain."

"Fine," his brother replied. "I could really care less about where we do this. But I do care about *when*. I'm not prepared to wait forever so you guys can train and practice. I can get everything set up within a week. So the day for these challenges will be this coming Saturday, the twenty-eighth. Until then, adios!"

Then Xavier conjured up a dust storm to take himself away.

Once Xavier was completely out of sight, Mr. Winchester put up his hand. He looked like an elementary school student who needed to ask his teacher for permission to go to the washroom.

"What? No high-fives for old guys?" he said with a big smile.

They all high-fived him, then each other. Xavier had fallen for their trick hook, line, and sinker.

CHAPTER 16

In order to increase their odds of successfully completing Xavier's challenges, Peter needed to convince Bradley to join their team again. Bradley didn't excel academically, but Peter knew he had a number of other traits that would be hugely beneficial. Bradley's strength, speed, and most of all his courage, would no doubt prove necessary.

Peter was pretty confident that Bradley would immediately jump at the opportunity to help. He figured that the *new* Bradley, the one who was more focused and serious about life now, would love the feeling of being a kid in a game again.

* * *

When Peter got home from school shortly past three o'clock on Monday, Bradley was in the garage, fussing around with his mountain bike. Bradley loved tinkering with stuff, especially his bike. He was in a constant struggle to make his already perfect bike even a little more perfect.

Maybe smoother. Or lighter. Or more shock absorbent.

"Petey boy!" Bradley said loudly as he noticed his little brother walking up the driveway. "Isn't this the most aerodynamic bike you've ever seen?"

"I have no clue about its aerodynamics," Peter said with a smile. "But if you let me take it out for a spin around the block, I'll tell you what I think."

"Nice try," Bradley replied. "But you know I never lend this bike to anyone. Not even you."

When Peter didn't head toward the house, which would be the natural thing to do when arriving home, Bradley noticed he was acting weird.

"What's up, dude?" he asked. "You need to borrow some money or something?"

"No," Peter replied, sitting down on one of the big storage boxes. He knew the explanation he was about to start was going to take a while. "Brad, Zoltan has a brother. An evil brother."

"Oh, c'mon," Bradley laughed. "Today is not April Fools' Day."

"Brad," Peter said with a serious look. "I know it sounds crazy, but it's true."

Peter spent the next fifteen minutes or so giving Bradley a condensed version of everything that had happened over the past two weeks. The more Peter spoke, the more Bradley became immersed in the tale.

"So I really need you on the team this Saturday," Peter said at the end of his explanation. "That way we'll have a chance against Xavier."

"Dude," Bradley replied right away. "Why didn't you tell me all this stuff earlier? Of course I'm in!"

Peter smiled and gave Bradley a high-five. Although he was relieved to have Bradley's help, there was no way he could mask how afraid he really was of being able to successfully complete every part of the plan...

CHAPTER 17

Peter, Nicola, Neil, and Bradley decided to gather at Mr. Winchester's home every afternoon for the rest of the week. Zoltan was still staying in the guest room and acting as if he weren't well enough to be on his own.

Shortly after the reunited team of four arrived on Tuesday, they expressed their reservations about being able to talk and plan without being spied on by Xavier.

"Xavier is a weather god, and nothing more," Mr. Winchester explained. "He can't see through walls or hear conversations from great distances."

"But he could," Bradley said, "sneak up and hide outside one of the windows, right? He'd be able to at least hear, or maybe even see what we're planning."

"Good point," Zoltan said. "He certainly could."

"I think I've got us mostly covered against that happening," Mr. Winchester explained. "My home has motion sensors outside, which would pick up someone approaching from any side of the house."

"And just to be safe," Peter (the excessive worrier) added, "we should make sure all doors and windows are closed and locked, and always keep the curtains shut."

"Smart ideas, Peter," Mr. Winchester replied. "And I would also suggest that we never, ever discuss these plans outside the confines of my home. Xavier could, in theory, be hiding behind any tree or sitting on any bench."

* * *

They knew their time was limited, so they went through as much as they could each afternoon. Today, which was Wednesday, Bradley couldn't come, as he had track and field practice until six.

Together with Mr. Winchester and Zoltan, they were slowly and tediously mapping out their plan. Peter liked to refer to this as the "dot the i's and cross the t's" stage.

* * *

About two hours later, which meant it was getting close to six o'clock, they figured it was time to call it a day and head home for dinner. Everyone, but most of all Peter, was exhausted. Preparing to save the world was much harder than it sounded.

"Tell you what," Peter said to Neil and Nicola as they walked to their bikes. "I'll buy you guys dinner tonight. My parents are going out for their anniversary and Sophia has ballet from five till seven, so I'm on my own for dinner anyway."

"Sure, how about pizza?" Nicola suggested.

"Good call, Nik," Neil replied immediately. "I've been cravin' some good 'za!"

* * *

They went to the small pizza shop on Third Avenue, the same one they'd been to so many times that the owner knew them all by name.

"Neil," Nicola said as they sat down at the open table in the far corner, "this sure feels like old times, doesn't it? I mean, hanging out with you when Claire isn't clinging to your arm."

"Yeah, it does feel a little weird," Neil admitted. "But as soon as we get through all of this trapping Xavier stuff and things go back to normal, I'll be hanging out with her as much as I can again."

"Speaking of Claire," Peter said, pointing at the door.

"Neil?" Claire said to him in shock. "What are you doing here?" Her face quickly began to turn red with rage. "You said you were going to Pete's house to do homework. But you're here! Having pizza? And Nik was invited, but not me?" Tears were beginning to form in her eyes.

"Hold up, baby," Neil said casually, hoping to quickly diffuse the situation. "It's not what you think..."

"Shut up!" she yelled at him. "You've been

acting weird for the last week or so. You never answer my calls. And when we do meet, you seem preoccupied with something. It's like you've always got somewhere else you'd rather be."

"Claire, baby," Neil said, a little more timidly than before. "It's just a misunderstanding."

"A misunderstanding!?" she yelled back, looking like she was about to hit him. I think I now know why you always get *Cs* in English. Think about it. You don't even know what the word *misunderstanding* means. This is not a misunderstanding. This is called *lying*. L-Y-I-N-G!"

She slammed the pizza shop door as she stormed out. The young clerk holding the two boxes of take-out pizza which her family had ordered by phone had no clue what to do or say.

Neil was shaken. Peter and Nicola quickly stood up to go over and console him, but he was in no mood to listen to any advice. In a bizarre trance, he opened the door and slowly started toward his bike.

CHAPTER 18

Neil looked like a zombie the next day at school. Peter knew what it felt like to stay up all night worrying, and gauging by the black bags under Neil's eyes, he had just had one of those nights. His poor friend was currently staring blankly at his open locker. With the first bell of the day set to ring in a few minutes, Peter figured now was his best chance to ask Neil how bad things were.

"She won't talk to me," Neil replied, still looking straight ahead. "She won't even look at me. And look at this note I just found in my locker."

He handed Peter the crushed piece of paper in his hand. There were only three words written on it:

We are over.

"I've been dumped, man," Neil said. "Plain and simple. Dumped."

Since Nicola was Peter's first girlfriend, and they were still together, he didn't know what it felt like to be dumped. But right now, he needed to think of something to say to his friend, and he needed to think of it quickly. Unfortunately for Peter, the only thing he came up with was something that he wished he hadn't.

"You shouldn't have lied to her," Peter said. "What were you thinking?"

Neil slammed his locker door hard and glared at Peter. "I lied to her," he said sharply, "to protect you and your little secret about the weather god stuff."

Peter didn't want this to escalate into an argument. But at the same time, he also wasn't prepared to take the blame for everything.

"I told you it was okay to tell Claire the truth," he said back to Neil. "It was you that decided not to. You said she'd never believe it, and that she would think you're a weirdo."

"Whatever," Neil said while walking away.

Peter noticed the all too familiar *butterflies in the stomach* feeling coming on.

"Pete, you dummy," he said to himself. "Why did you just say that?"

The bell had already started to ring, so Peter jogged toward his English class. On the inside, he knew he was going to spend the entire day playing through countless scenarios of how to smooth things over with Neil.

CHAPTER 19

Peter lay down on the sofa the instant he got home from school. He was emotionally exhausted. He had spent the entire day trying to figure out when and how to approach Neil, but ended up doing nothing. Now it was a quarter past three, and his worrying was only set to continue.

"Should've talked to him after P.E." Peter mumbled to himself. "There was no one close by in the change room. That was my best chance."

Peter's cycle of worrying always went something like this: Make a mistake. Regret it. Think endlessly about how to undo it. Do nothing. Worry more.

His mom had told him numerous times that he would give himself an ulcer by the age of eighteen if he didn't learn how to relax more and stop obsessing.

"Catch!" Bradley said as he came around the corner into the room, passing a basketball that Peter wasn't expecting.

"Ouch!" Peter yelped as the ball smacked him hard in the chest.

"You still suck at b-ball," Bradley laughed. "C'mon, let's play a game of twenty-one or something."

Back when Bradley was fourteen, he had decided that becoming a rich and famous basketball player was in the cards for his future. He had somehow managed to convince their parents to spend a few hundred bucks on a regulation height hoop for their driveway. Up until last year, Bradley and his buddies used to use it all the time. They would crank up the volume of whatever cheesy rock song was popular, and take turns trying to show off their moves to each other. They put even more effort into displaying their skills whenever a girl their age happened to be walking by. But now that Bradley was at college, and actually taking his education seriously for the first time ever, the hoop rarely got used.

"I'll give you a ten-point lead," Bradley begged, desperately needing an opponent to play against. "And if you beat me, I'll do all your chores this weekend."

Everyone knew Bradley was a great athlete, as his name often appeared in the local paper for winning this or setting a new record in that. But few people knew that Bradley also had an amazing ability to read peoples' emotions. Peter's current expression tipped off Bradley to the fact that something was wrong.

"Something happen with Nik?" he asked Peter while picking up the basketball and sitting down beside him.

"No, actually it's about Neil," Peter replied. "Claire dumped him."

"Ouch, that sucks," Bradley said. "Why? What did he do?"

Peter spent the next ten minutes explaining everything to Bradley. At first, he thought it was a *funny and cute* little tale of teenage love. But once he realized that Neil might be so upset that he wouldn't want to help them defeat Xavier, his expression quickly changed.

"Petey," Bradley said to him. "You may be smart, but you've got no tact."

"Tact?" Peter asked.

"Hey," Bradley went on. "Neil still got that part-time job at the veggie shop on Fifth Avenue?"

"Yeah," Peter answered. "Wait. You're not gonna go there by yourself and try talking to him, are you?"

Bradley paused for a few seconds, thinking carefully about what Peter had just asked. "No, I'm not," he replied. Then he got up and quickly left the room. A minute or two later, Peter heard the car engine start, and watched through the window as Bradley backed out of the driveway.

CHAPTER 20

The plan was for everyone to meet up at Mr. Winchester's house on Friday afternoon to review (for the umpteenth time) all the fine details for the big day tomorrow. Peter and Nicola arrived by bike first, and Bradley drove in shortly after. Considering all that Neil had been through in the last two days, Peter thought the chances of him coming today were extremely slim, or more likely, zero.

"Don't worry, Petey," Bradley said with confidence. "He'll show."

"What did you do?" Peter asked, sounding quite concerned. "You didn't threaten to beat him up if he didn't come, did you?"

"Threaten him?" Bradley laughed. "No, I did much better than that."

"Yo!" Neil yelled loudly while riding up. "Sorry I'm late. I dropped by Claire's house on my way here."

"Really?" Nicola asked. "You mean she's not

angry at you anymore?"

Bradley walked up to Neil and gave him a big high-five.

"Thanks again, Brad," Neil said. "I owe you big time."

"Can someone please explain what's going on here?" Nicola asked with a smile.

"I'd love to," Bradley said, as if he'd been waiting for someone to ask him that exact question. "Yesterday, after promising Petey that I wouldn't go to see Neil *by myself*, I set out on a mission to get Claire and Neil back together."

"You what?" Nicola asked. "But how did you know it would work?"

"Well, if there's one thing I learned from living with Petey all these years," Bradley continued, "it's that an *organized* plan almost always succeeds. So anyway, after Pete filled me in on what happened at the pizza shop, I drove straight to Claire's house. I used to be friends with her brother Chris, like way back in Grade 5 or 6, so I know where she lives. I rang the doorbell, and when she answered I gave her that DVD of Zoltan demonstrating his powers and begged her to watch it. You know, the one we all watched two years ago. Then I waited outside on the front steps while she reluctantly watched it."

"You mean she didn't invite you inside?" Peter asked.

"She was home alone," Bradley replied. "So

that would've been weird. After she watched it, she came back outside. But she had that deer in the headlights look on her face. I explained everything to her, you know, all about the weather gods and stuff. I told her what we did two years ago, and about what's going on now."

"And?" Nicola jumped in, eager for Bradley to get to the good part.

"And she felt so bad after hearing the whole story," Bradley went on, "that she wanted to see Neil and forgive him as soon as possible. I drove her over to the veggie shop where Neil works, and left her in the car while I went in and bought two boxes of apples. I asked Neil to help carry one back to my car, and when he got there, voila! There was Claire, waiting for him with open arms! I didn't feel like watching all the lovey-dovey stuff, so I went for a jog in the park behind the shopping mall. And when I came back fifteen minutes later, Claire said all was good!"

"You cupid!" Nicola remarked, lightly punching Bradley on the shoulder. "You got them back together!"

"And Claire even offered to help us out," Neil added.

"Cool," Peter said while nodding. "I mean, cool about both things. About you guys getting back together, and that she's happy to help."

CHAPTER 21

After allowing everyone a little more time for chitchat, plus some time to joke around with Zoltan, Mr. Winchester suggested they all congregate in the living room to go through everything one final time.

He looked over at Peter, Neil, Nicola, and Bradley in utter amazement. Wow, they sure had grown up a lot in two years. He wasn't focusing on the increase in their height, but more on how mature they all had become. He could still recall the first time he met Peter, the geeky puzzle-loving kid who was teased at school and had very few friends. But the Peter standing in front of him now was beaming with pride and looked more than ready for what lay ahead tomorrow.

"Peter," Mr. Winchester said, slowly standing up. "I'm not going to pretend that I'm in charge this time. I may be the eldest, but you are the leader. Thanks to all your hard work, and the help of your talented and dedicated friends, I can say, with complete confidence, this plan will work."

"I'll second that!" Bradley said, turning to give Neil another high-five.

"Any last words of wisdom, then?" Mr. Winchester asked Peter. "Or any final changes we need to know about?"

Peter's emotions could turn on a dime, and he could feel his throat growing tighter. He didn't want to start fumbling his words or crying in front of everyone right now, but it looked as if that was going to be unavoidable. He turned around to gather his composure, and then spun back to look at his team.

"To quote one of the cheesiest phrases I've ever heard," Peter said. "A chain is only as strong as its weakest link."

"Well, that's definitely me!" Bradley joked. "At least as far as brains go."

"No," Peter replied, his voice a little shaky. "We have no weak links. None. Zero. Zilch. This plan WILL work. I am certain of it." Peter started to choke up, to the point that he could hardly get the right words out. "We'll meet some smags, oops, I mean some *snags* along the way. But we are all capable of figuring out how to deal with them."

Peter then reached into his backpack and pulled out three small boxes. "Here you go, guys," he said while passing them out. "Remember when you three pitched in to buy me that watch two years back? Well, I went out and bought all three of you digital watches. Wait, that sounds like I spent a lot of money, which I didn't. I found them at one of those shops where they sell used clothes and stuff, so they cost like next to nothing. Anyway, they are all synchronized, to the second."

"Petey the perfectionist!" Bradley said while putting the watch on his left wrist. "You've thought of everything, haven't you?"

"My first ever watch!" Neil said excitedly. "But I guess I'll have no excuse for being late for school anymore."

Peter smiled. Only Neil could make a group of people laugh without having had the slightest intention of doing so.

CHAPTER 22

The next day, September 28, the day which Xavier had set for the challenges, Peter and his team arrived at Silverhead Mountain about fifteen minutes earlier than Xavier had told them to be there.

They now stood staring down the path which led to the ruins, the exact same place they'd been standing at two years ago to start Zoltan's challenges.

"So what's the drill?" Bradley asked, since he hadn't been there for the start of the challenges two years ago.

"Last time we just walked to the end of this path, and a note was waiting on a tree for us," Peter replied.

Peter and Nicola were leading the way, hand in hand. Bradley and Neil followed behind them, making childish comments about the lovebirds in front of them.

After putting up with their remarks for a minute or so, Nicola spun around. "Would you guys grow up?" she joked. "Especially you, Neil. You and Claire are stuck to each other like white on rice!"

When she turned to face forward again, they were now close enough to see the end of the path. But instead of a note on a tree, Xavier was waiting for them in person.

"I've never been one for pleasantries," Xavier said in a low and monotone voice. "And since we all know why you are here, let's just get on with it."

No one replied. There wasn't really anything that needed to be said.

"But at least make it interesting for me to watch," Xavier continued, with a cruel grin on his face. "Don't go and fail on the first one. Then I would have wasted so much time preparing puzzles two through five!" He turned around quickly. "This way, KIDS!"

Peter and Nicola looked back to face Neil and Bradley. All four of them shrugged their shoulders, and then began to follow Xavier.

Peter's anxiety was somewhere up in the stratosphere right now. But a teeny tiny part of him was actually excited. There was still that little kid inside him that LOVED the challenge of a new puzzle.

CHAPTER 23

Xavier led them into an open chamber, which was roughly half the size of a school gymnasium. The only thing in the room was a cage, which was on the floor right in the middle. It looked like something that would be used to transport a tiger or lion from one zoo to another. There was a thick chain attached to the top of the cage, and as their eyes followed the chain up, they saw where it disappeared into a hole in the ceiling.

"You've gotta be kidding me," Peter said. "We are going to have to lock ourselves in there, aren't we?"

Neil took the note taped to the open cage door and went to hand it to Peter. No one really needed to read it, as they were pretty sure about what it would say.

"May I do the honors?" Bradley asked, snatching the note from Neil before it got to Peter's hand. He unfolded it and read its short contents aloud.

Go in the cage and close the door behind you. You'll hear the click when it locks.

"Pretty pointless note," Bradley said while crushing it into a ball. "We could've figured out that much on our own."

They cautiously stepped into the cage, which easily had enough room for all of them. But the top of the cage only came up to Peter's shoulders, so they had to crouch once inside.

"First time in a cell, Petey?" Bradley joked.

* * *

Bradley had stayed in jail, very briefly, a few months back. He and his friends were held there under suspicion of drunk and disorderly conduct after a night out. But Bradley and his friends hadn't been drinking, nor had they been looking for trouble. They actually had just been trying to be good Samaritans. While walking back to their car after watching a movie, they had spotted a group of drunk losers hassling a couple of girls outside a convenience store. The drunks took offence when Bradley told them to *leave the girls alone and go home*, and their group quickly jumped Bradley and his friends. Luckily, drunks are easy to outrun, so no one was hurt too badly. But the cops were called and they decided to hold everyone involved overnight while they investigated the incident. The next morning, after the police had spoken to several witnesses, they apologized to Bradley's group and released them.

* * *

They heard the sound of metal on metal, and then watched as the chain began to move. The cage was slowly being raised off the ground. Peter and his team had to grab hold of the bars to keep themselves from falling over.

About thirty seconds later, when it looked like they were about a meter off the ground, the cage stopped.

A digital timer on the wall, which they hadn't noticed before, was set to countdown from five minutes. But for some reason, it hadn't started yet.

"Guess Xavier is a little slow on the ball, eh?" Bradley said softly. "He forgot to start the timer."

Just as Bradley finished his comment, the entrance door opened again and in walked Xavier.

"You didn't think I'd lock you in there without the key, did you?" he laughed.

Xavier dropped the key, which was attached to a large key ring, on the ground in front of his feet. Then he turned around and walked back out the same door. As soon as the door closed behind him, the timer started.

"But how are we supposed to reach the key?" Nicola asked. "It's way too far away. And there's nothing in here that can help us."

"Yeah," Neil added. "It's gotta be at least, like, two or three meters away."

Peter had played the crane game at the arcade many, many times. What they were dealing with now was more or less the same, in principle. Or one could compare it to fishing off a pier: something Peter did every year when he visited his grandparents.

"What we need to do is fashion together something that can reach that far," Peter said. "And put some kind of hook on the end."

"Well, we all brought our jackets," Nicola suggested. "Why don't we tie them all together?"

"Roger that," Bradley said, saluting Nicola. Bradley much preferred the manual labor to the thinking. "And while I do that, someone come up with a way to make a hook."

"That's a cinch!" Peter said right away, reaching into his backpack.

He pulled out the cutlery case from the bottom. Peter always took his knife, fork, and spoon everywhere he went. One reason was that he didn't like the environmental impact of using disposable ones at fast food shops. But even more than that, he absolutely hated it when he picked up a utensil at a restaurant with food caked on it.

"Sorry, Mr. Fork," Peter said to his utensil. "It's been nice knowing you."

He bent the fork into a U-shape. Bradley and

Neil had just finished tying the jackets together, so Peter attached his "hook" to the end of the last sleeve using some string he had brought with him.

"Time to go fishin'!" Neil announced like a hillbilly.

They should have been more concerned about the timer on the wall, but they all seemed very calm and cool. It was as if they knew their plan was going to succeed.

"Let me give it a go," Bradley said, ready to show how his years of sports made him the ideal candidate to do this.

He held one end of the *rope made of jackets* in his left hand, and tossed the hooked end in the direction of the key. Unfortunately, it didn't land even remotely close. This task was apparently going to be much harder than they all thought. He quickly reeled it back in and made a second attempt. A little closer than the first, but nowhere near close enough.

"You've gotta aim past the key," Peter advised, "and then try to hook the ring as you pull it back."

"I know. I know," Bradley said impatiently, already getting frustrated with himself.

His third throw was perfect. The fork bounced once and then came to a stop just beyond the key. He carefully pulled it back, trying to make sure the fork was lined up to slide into and grab the key ring. But the fork was upside down, so even though it slid over the right spot, it didn't hook the ring.

"This isn't working, guys," Nicola said. "If we had hours, we'd probably get it, but—"

"But we don't," Neil said, finishing her sentence for her. "In fact, we've only got two minutes and eighteen seconds to go."

Peter felt the initial stage of panic start to set in. He knew these sensations all too well: sweaty palms, racing heart, slight dizziness, shortness of breath.

"Deep breaths," he said softly to himself. He couldn't afford to have a full-fledged panic attack right now.

Bradley was getting angrier and angrier. He dropped the jacket pile and began kicking at the cage bars. He looked like a three-year-old having a temper tantrum. Needless to say, this caused the cage to shake, which in turn distracted the rest of them from thinking.

"Stop that!" Nicola yelled sharply at him. "You don't think you're strong enough to kick your way out of here, do you?!"

Neil spun around. From the expression on his face, he had just had a stroke of genius. "When the odds are stacked against you," he said with a smirk on his face, "you call the Neilster."

"Dude, if you have an idea," Bradley said sharply, still unable to shake off his own frustration, "spit it out."

Neil put his hands on the bar closest to where he was standing.

"Let me guess," Bradley said sarcastically. "The *Neilster* is going to bend the bars with his bare hands?"

"Ignore Brad," Peter said to Neil supportively. "C'mon, let's hear your idea."

"Well, what I'm thinking," Neil continued, speaking quickly, "is that maybe the cage was built with a couple of bars that were intentionally not welded in place."

"Huh?" Bradley said rudely.

"You know how cages are built," Neil continued, ignoring Bradley. "The bars are inserted into the holes in the thick frame, and then welded."

"So maybe a couple of the bars can be lifted up and slid out!" Nicola said excitedly.

They each took a side, hoping to find a loose bar or two that could be removed.

"No dice," Peter said. "Anyone?"

The other three had the same result. The timer had just reached fifty-nine seconds. They were almost out of time.

"Hold on," Neil said. "I've got another idea. Righty tighty. Lefty loosey!"

"Righty what?" Bradley asked.

"Quickly Neil!" Nicola said in a panic. "We've only got forty seconds left."

"Twisting screws or lids to the left loosens them," Neil explained. "Maybe a couple of the bars can be unscrewed and removed from the frame."

With no time to spare, and no other suggestions, they all began quickly checking the bars.

"Bingo!" Bradley yelled about ten seconds later.

The two bars in front of him could be twisted. Neil came over to help, and he and Bradley twisted like crazy until the bars came loose.

"Only eighteen seconds to go!" Nicola announced. "C'mon! Let's go!"

One by one, they squeezed through the gap and jumped to the floor. The last one out, Peter, hit the ground when the timer read 0:04.

Before they could start celebrating, Xavier walked through the door.

With no expression on his face, he looked directly into Peter's eyes. "You can consider that first challenge an easy warm-up for you and your team," he said coldly. "Now the real tests begin."

CHAPTER 24

Xavier led them through a long, winding, seemingly endless corridor to get to their next challenge. "Don't tell me," he said, looking back at Peter and his team, "that you are expecting the rest to be so easy?"

Peter had strictly instructed his team to never speak to Xavier during their challenges today, even if they were being asked a direct question.

"Cat got your tongues?" Xavier said loudly, unimpressed by the silent treatment he was getting. "Here are the instructions for your second challenge. Read them carefully."

Xavier handed the note to Peter, but he decided not to look at it until Xavier had left the room.

Just like their first challenge, they were in another chamber of roughly the same size, and there was nothing inside it other than what was going to be used for the challenge.

At the far end of the room, there was an empty

wooden barrel. Well, it wasn't a complete barrel, it was only the bottom half of one. Xavier must have cut it in half in order to set up the challenge. Beside the barrel was a garden hose, hooked up to a faucet. Just behind the barrel and hose, there was a staircase, which looked like it rose to roughly the same height as a basketball net. The staircase led up to some sort of loft or platform.

With Xavier no longer in sight, Peter unfolded the note.

> *Fill the barrel with water up to the red line, which as you can see, is about a finger length below the rim. The challenge is to carry the barrel to the top of the stairs. Sure, it'll be heavy, but the four of you can certainly manage it. But here's the catch: If you accidently spill any of the water, even one drop, then you fail. And for this challenge, you may make four attempts.*

"Where does he come up with this stuff?" Neil asked, shaking his head.

Bradley had already turned on the hose and was filling up the barrel. As the water slowly rose, Peter got down on his hands and knees to get a closer look.

The first thing he saw was the *110 Liter* black stamp. Since that was the stamp for a full barrel, a half barrel would hold 55 liters. And the red line being about ten centimeters below the rim meant they'd probably only have to put in about 45 liters. That converted to roughly 45 kilograms, plus he had to add the weight of the barrel itself. Once he'd finished his calculations, he figured the combined weight of water and barrel would be pretty close to his own body weight.

Due to the reddish stains covering the entire inside of the barrel, Peter guessed that it had contained red wine at some point in the past. But kegs like this were typically moved around using trollies, so there were no handles or grip holds. The only way to lift it was going to be by getting their fingers under the bottom.

"There we go," said Bradley. "Got the water up to the red line."

"This is going to be pretty awkward to lift," Peter said. "But I think as long as we move in sync, we should be able to do it without spilling any water."

They took their places around the barrel.

"On the count of three," Peter said. "One, two, three!"

The water-filled barrel was heavier than they thought. They groaned and grunted while slowly lifting it off the ground. Just before they had it high enough to be able to straighten their knees, it wobbled a bit and some water splashed over the side.

"Lower it down slowly," Peter instructed.

"Guys, I think that was my fault," Nicola said. "My wrist started hurting and I tried to adjust my grip."

Bradley grabbed the hose and topped up the water. "It wasn't your fault, Nik," he said supportively.

"What we need," Neil suggested, "is something flat, like a board, to put underneath it. Xavier never said we couldn't use stuff like that."

It was almost as if a magician had been listening to Neil, because suddenly they spotted a wooden board, which was about the size of the top of a coffee table, leaning against the far wall of the room. Since they all knew the chamber had been empty, except for the barrel, when they entered the room, they had no explanation for the board's appearance now.

They carefully managed to slide the board under the barrel without spilling any water. This was going to make it way easier to lift and carry.

Once again, on the count of three, they lifted. It was still heavy, but they were able to get their legs straight without too much trouble. Next, they shuffled to the bottom of the stairs. Peter and Nicola climbed up backward, so that Neil and Bradley, the two strongest, could support the bulk of the weight while facing toward the steps.

"Man, this thing gets heavier by the second," Neil said, face purple from straining so hard.

"Don't wimp out now," Bradley said, in a half-sincere and half-sarcastic tone.

They were almost halfway up when Neil's shaking caused a bit of water to splash out.

"No!" Bradley yelled. "We were so close!"

They tipped the barrel and dumped the rest of the water out over the side of the stairs. There was no sense in wasting valuable energy carrying a full barrel back down.

"I think the problem was that we tried to do it all in one go," Nicola said.

"You're right, Nik," Peter added. "Xavier never said we couldn't put it down to rest while climbing the steps. Why don't we put the end Nik and I are carrying down every couple of steps? Then we take your places and support it for a while so you guys can rest your arms. When you're ready, we all go back to our original spots, and we do a couple more steps."

It took close to five minutes to fill up the barrel for their third attempt. Neil was lying on his back, arms aching from the last try. Bradley was swinging his arms in big circles, hoping to improve his circulation as much as possible.

Once everyone was sufficiently rested, they began their third attempt. They decided to take breaks every two steps, and by doing so, everyone seemed to be managing just fine. It was going magnificently.

"Only two more to go," Nicola said happily.

"We're almost there."

"Shhh," said Neil. "Don't jinx it."

But it was too late. It had just been jinxed. Peter wobbled a little, and that jolt was just enough to make some water slosh and then spill over.

"You've gotta be kidding me!" Bradley yelled in frustration. "We only had two steps left!"

They dumped out the rest of the water, and descended the stairs in silence. They would all need a fair amount of rest before their final attempt.

Angry with himself for screwing up at such an inopportune time, Peter turned on the hose to refill the barrel, and then quietly walked a few meters away from everyone. He kept his back facing them in order to avoid making any eye contact.

Bradley and Neil were both lying on their backs, breathing heavily. Meanwhile, Nicola was sitting on the bottom step wishing she hadn't unintentionally jinxed Peter.

"Alright, Petey. Let's do this," Bradley said, walking over and patting Peter on the back. "No point in sulking. It's not going to make this last attempt any easier."

They got into position again. And they all looked very, very serious. They were all business.

"On the count of three," Bradley said. "We got this, guys. One, two—"

"Hold on, hold on," Peter said suddenly. Thankfully, no one had started to lift yet.

Peter took a couple of steps back and removed the note from his pocket. From the expression on his face, it was clear that Peter was having some sort of brainwave. The other three quietly sat down and faced away from him, to give him space to think.

"When we started this challenge," Peter said quietly to himself, "Xavier told us to read the note carefully. Carefully. He wouldn't have specifically said *carefully* if there wasn't something in the note we needed to spot."

Peter read the note over and over, mumbling away the whole time.

Nicola watched her boyfriend in awe. No matter how complicated or confusing a problem was, Peter would never, ever consider throwing in the towel. The world needed more *Peters*.

"Let me take a look at it," Nicola said after walking over and putting her arm around him. Peter, happy for the help and support, passed the note to Nicola and then kept pacing around.

"No hidden message?" Neil asked him.

"Not that I could see," he answered.

Nicola was awful at math and science, but she always got As in English. Apparently, it depends on which side of one's brain is dominant. If there was something hidden in the words of this note, Nicola was by far the most qualified to find it.

Nicola and Peter certainly had different ways of concentrating. Nicola stood in one spot and silently looked at the note. Peter, on the other hand, paced around endlessly. He was currently doing a weird figure eight pattern, where he'd keep going around the barrel and then step over the hose. When he tried to spin around too quickly, he tripped over the hose and fell.

"You okay, Pete?" Bradley asked, although it was obvious that the only thing Peter had hurt was his pride.

"I'm fine," he replied. "I accidentally tripped over that stupid hose."

Nicola's face lit up. "Xavier, you tricky little…" she said. "And you thought we'd never notice."

"Notice what?" Bradley asked.

HI READER! (^_^)
NICOLA JUST FIGURED IT OUT! CAN YOU?

"Listen again to the note," she continued. "*But if you accidentally spill any of the water…* Accidentally. Accidentally."

"Not following you," Neil said, clearly needing a more accurate explanation.

"That word is the trick, or hidden message, or whatever you want to call it," she explained. "Think about it. On our first three attempts, we accidentally spilled some water, right? But what if we spill it *intentionally*? All of it. You know, just tip it over and pour it all out. Then all we'd have to do is carry the empty barrel up the stairs."

"But that would be too easy," said Neil, thinking she was trying to create a solution out of nothing.

"Yeah, that sounds sketchy to me too," Bradley added. "But it's your call Petey. You're in charge here."

"No, it's Nik's call," Peter said right away. "She's the one who spotted it. If she thinks it's worth going for, then I'm with her. One hundred percent."

"Well, I can't say I'm one hundred percent sure," she said, sounding slightly less confident than before. "But I'm pretty sure it'll work."

Bradley and Neil pushed the barrel over. Once all the water was out, Peter took a towel from his backpack and wiped it until it was bone dry.

Satisfied that every last drop was gone, Peter gave Bradley and Neil the okay to carry the barrel up the stairs. It was light enough now that this task was a breeze. When they reached the top, they slammed it down hard.

The entrance door opened and Xavier walked in. He looked a little flustered. It was obvious from his expression that he certainly hadn't expected them to find the word trick he'd hidden in the note.

"Follow me," he mumbled. "And wipe off those smug grins. The next one is way harder."

CHAPTER 25

Their third challenge looked similar to a place at the big mall in Stoneburg where Peter had spent countless hours playing while his parents shopped. Their family called it the *ball room* or the *ball pool* or the *ball pit*. Just like at the mall in Stoneburg, they were now standing in front of a large square pit, about half the size of a swimming pool, filled with thousands and thousands of baseball-sized, hollow plastic balls.

"Petey," Bradley said. "I used to love going to the ball pit. Man, this takes me back." He looked like he was getting ready to dive in.

"Wait," Nicola said, sounding a bit concerned. "You don't wanna hurt yourself."

"Hurt myself?" Bradley laughed. "By landing on a pile of light plastic balls? C'mon, you know what these things are like. When you land on them, it's like falling down on a mattress."

Bradley jumped high in the air, spread his arms and legs, and did a belly flop into the colorful balls.

"Can someone remind me how old he is?" Peter asked while watching this childish display.

Less than a second after Bradley landed, numerous holes opened up in the ceiling, and more balls started to fall into the pit.

"Brad, get out of there! Quick!" Peter yelled.

Bradley was already pretty close to the ledge, so it only took him a few seconds to get there. The instant his hand touched the ledge, the holes in the ceiling closed, putting an end to the falling balls.

They heard some footsteps. They looked up, and as they had expected, Xavier was standing on the ledge on the opposite side of the ball pit.

"Allow me to explain," he announced loudly. "The rules are fairly simple. All four of you have to get over here, to this ledge where I am standing, in twenty-five seconds or less. And that doesn't mean twenty-five seconds per person. The timer starts the instant someone enters the pit. And then all four of you have to get to this ledge before the twenty-five seconds elapse. And as you just saw, balls will fall from above while you're moving through the pit. I figured it would make it a little more, I don't know, let's say... fun to watch?"

"Twenty-five seconds?" Bradley asked. "That's way too short."

"Stop whining," Xavier barked back. "It's more

than ample. And before I forget, for this challenge, you get only three attempts."

Since he was in no mood to field any more questions, Xavier turned around and walked out the door behind him.

"He can't be serious about the time limit," Bradley said. "I mean, I might have a chance, if I take a big runup first. But, and no offense, the rest of you aren't really big athletes or anything."

They took a few minutes to scan both the ball pit and the ledge that led up to the start of the pit. It was just under three meters from the wall to the ledge. That would be enough space to get some pretty good momentum before leaping in. But making forward progress through the balls was going to be the hard part. It was probably so deep that their feet wouldn't reach the bottom. That meant they were going to have to *swim* through the balls to get across. Not an easy thing to do.

"Pete," Nicola said nervously, squeezing his hand hard. "This looks really tough."

"Yeah, it does," he replied, trying to mask how scared he really was. *Scared* was a drastic understatement. Peter was absolutely, utterly terrified.

* * *

Back when Peter was five and a half, which meant he was old enough to enter the mall's ball pit as long as a parent or responsible sibling was with him, he had one of the most traumatic events of his life. While his parents were shopping with Sophia, he and Bradley were allowed to play in the ball pit. Bradley had promised to stay close by and keep an eye on his younger brother the entire time.

When his parents finished shopping and came back to fetch the two boys, Peter was nowhere to be found. Bradley had been enjoying himself so much that he had long since forgotten his duty to be watching his little brother.

Everyone just figured that Peter probably became bored, got out, and went to one of the two hobby shops in the mall. He loved looking at the puzzles and games in both shops, and could do so for hours on end. But a search of those two shops, followed by the rest of the mall, yielded nothing. A few announcements were then made, but Peter still couldn't be found.

Peter was actually stuck at the bottom of the ball pit. Physically, he was completely fine. He could breathe, and he had no injuries. But as soon as he realized that he was stuck, he got scared and peed his pants. And he was so embarrassed about people seeing him that he decided not to call for help.

By this point, everyone was getting quite concerned, as of course they should be when a child suddenly vanishes. The ball pit staff, who were just a couple of lazy high school kids, ordered everyone out. Then his parents and Bradley started calling out to him, asking if he could hear them. Peter knew he didn't want to spend the rest of his life soaked in pee at the bottom of the Stoneburg Mall ball pit, so he decided to respond. The staff then carefully followed his voice until they located him and pulled him out safely.

Finally out, Peter lied about what had happened. He said he had fallen asleep, and had no idea how long he'd been down there. That way no one would ever know how much of a chicken he really was.

* * *

But like it or not, Peter needed to push that awful memory aside.

"Well, how's this for starters?" Neil suggested. "If we all take a big runup and leap at the same time, then we'll all have the full twenty-five seconds to use."

"That might work," Peter replied, still half stuck in his flashback. "But moving forward in those balls is harder than you think."

"Why don't we use our first attempt," Nicola suggested, "to gauge how hard it's gonna be?"

They spent a couple minutes figuring out the ideal place and position to start running from. It was time to give it a go.

"Ladies and gentlemen," Bradley said in a deep voice. "Start your engines."

"You know the drill," Neil said next. "On three. One, two, three!"

They all simultaneously sprinted toward the ball pit, and jumped at more or less the same time. Bradley, of course, launched himself way further than anyone else. Once in the ball pit, while balls rained down from above, they flailed and scrambled to get across as quickly as possible. Bradley was making good time and Neil was doing fairly well. But Peter and Nicola were pretty much going nowhere, almost like cars spinning their wheels on ice.

Bradley could see the end. He spun around and yelled to Neil. "Neil! We gotta help them across! Grab whoever is closest to you and pull them along!"

But the hailstorm of balls falling from the ceiling made it difficult to see Peter and Nicola clearly.

Neil finally managed to spot Peter, and Bradley found Nicola. They did their best to try to get them moving forward, but it wasn't helping enough.

A loud buzzer sounded, and the holes in the ceiling closed, stopping any more balls from falling.

Xavier was standing on the ledge they had been trying to reach.

"You weren't even close!" he laughed. "You guys are pathetic."

Bradley got ready to throw a couple balls at Xavier, but Peter quickly grabbed his wrist before he had a chance to do so.

"Save your energy," he said softly to Bradley.

They slowly made their way back to the start, hopped out, and sat down on the ledge. After at least two or three minutes of silence, Neil offered up a suggestion.

"How about this?" he said. "Brad and I launch Nik as far as we can. You know, like we throw her in. Then we quickly jump in after."

"And what about Pete?" Nicola asked.

"Pete can make it across fine on his own," Bradley said, hoping to insert some confidence into his little brother. "You got this, Pete. Right?"

"Suppose I don't really have a choice," Peter mumbled. "But yeah, I'll go for it."

"But timing is everything if we do it this way," Neil continued. "We will swing Nik back and forth. Then Pete starts his run up. And just as he leaps in, we launch Nik."

"I think it'll work," Bradley said. "But you and I have gotta move like lightning the second we let go of Nik. By the time we go back to get a runup and then jump in, we'll be at least five or six seconds behind them."

Everyone got into position. Peter was crouched down at the wall, like a sprinter at the start line. Nicola lay down by the ledge of the ball pit. Neil took her wrists, and Bradley her ankles. They lifted her up and started swinging her back and forth.

"Okay, Pete," Neil said loudly. "You start running on two. One, two."

Peter bolted for the ball pit.

"Three!" Neil yelled. He and Bradley sent Nicola soaring just as Peter was leaving the ground.

Peter had never had such a perfect jump in his life. It was most certainly one for the record books. Neil and Bradley scrambled to the wall and then ran and jumped. But the balls were raining down hard from above, so it was tough for them to see how far they'd actually gone.

"I made it!" Nicola yelled as she touched the far ledge.

"I think I'm almost there too," Peter said a few seconds later. "Yeah. I can see it!"

But when Peter was within the last meter of the wall, the bell sounded and the balls stopped falling again. Peter and Bradley were both very close to the end, but Neil still had at least two body lengths to go.

Exhausted, they all lay down on top of the balls. They knew Xavier was standing on the ledge looking at them, but they chose to avoid making any eye contact with him.

"Sorry, guys," Neil said. "I slipped during take-off. That's why I only got this far. But don't worry, I'll be fine next time."

Bradley looked flustered. He wasn't angry at Neil, but at himself. He had been the top athlete in school for all of his junior high and high school years, but he had just failed to complete what seemed like an easy challenge. He hated losing. Really, really hated it.

"I don't know, guys," Bradley said. "I had a perfect jump, and I was moving along pretty fast. But I still didn't make it. I might be able to go a little quicker, but not much."

They went back to the start again and lay on the ledge to catch their breath. They only had one more shot at this, so they couldn't waste it.

"Don't look so down," Nicola said to the boys. "We were super close. I'm sure with a little luck, we'll get there on our next try."

"But to quote my little brother," Bradley said. "When the odds are extremely against you, you have to find a way to improve them."

"I just wish there was a way to shut off the balls raining down from above," Neil said.

"No kidding," Peter added. "Then at least we could make sure we are moving in a straight line."

A fairly long period of silence ensued. With no new ideas about how to do anything differently, it looked like all they could do was hope for a whole lot of luck on try number three."

"I wonder how many balls are in there in total?" Neil asked absent-mindedly. "I mean, you think eventually the stock in the ceiling would run out. He can't have an endless supply."

Peter looked at Neil. But nothing needed to be said. By the expression on Peter's face it was obvious he was on to something.

"How could I have overlooked that?" Peter said while beginning to stand up. "Look at the ball pit. Notice how the balls have never overflowed? But they should be overflowing. He's dumped thousands of balls from above."

"So?" Bradley said.

"Well there's only one possibility then," Peter continued. "When the balls start dropping from the ceiling, some sort of hole must open up in the bottom of the ball pit. That's why the level always stays the same."

"And you want us to find that hole, right?" Nicola asked.

"Actually, I think I already know where it is," Peter replied quickly. "Look right out there. About a body length in front of me. See where the balls are a little lower than the rest?"

"Yeah, the shape kind of looks like a mini-whirlpool," Neil said.

"The hole that the balls are exiting through is right below it," Peter said. "I'm willing to bet it's big enough for a person to fit through. And I also think once we drop through it, there will be a path to some stairs that lead directly to the opposite ledge."

"Sounds a little over the top to me," Bradley said. "I think our best chance is to do the same thing as last time, but just do it flawlessly."

"But you just said," Peter reminded his brother, "that we need a new way."

"I'm with Pete on this one," Nicola said in support of Peter. "I mean, like, how many times has he been wrong?"

"Well, not that many, I suppose," Bradley answered. "Okay, I'm cool with it. Pete, let's hear how we play this."

Peter outlined what to do for their final attempt. He would jump in feet first, and land exactly where he believed the hole to be. As soon as he felt himself getting sucked out along with the balls, he'd yell for the next person to jump.

He got them to stand behind him in single file, and stressed how important is was for them to remember the exact spot they were aiming for. Peter knew that once he jumped in, the falling balls would make it extremely difficult for the other three to see where they were jumping.

All things considered, Peter was remarkably calm. He had enormous faith in math and physics, and he was sure this plan would work. Peter recalled watching the sand pass through the narrow part of the egg timer his mom used while boiling eggs. They were about to do more or less the same thing with their bodies right now.

Peter took a short runup, jumped high, and his

feet hit the exact spot he was aiming for. A couple seconds later, he felt himself being pulled down along with the balls. "Nik, now!" he yelled.

Nicola did the same as Peter. Neil and Bradley were both ready and waiting for their turns.

Peter felt his speed accelerate as he dropped through the hole onto the landing area below. The staircase to the opposite ledge, the exact thing he had been hoping for, was right in front of him.

"I was right!" he yelled, even though he knew no one could hear him.

He bolted for the stairs. He didn't want to be in the way when then rest of his team started dropping out of the hole.

Nicola, followed by Neil, and finally Bradley, dropped through in rapid succession. They too saw the staircase, plus they could hear Peter screaming for them to hurry.

When Bradley reached the top of the stairs, meaning all four were now on the ledge they had been heading for, the bell still hadn't sounded. They had made it in time.

"YES!" Bradley yelled as if he'd just hit the jackpot. "Take that, Xavier!"

Peter quickly hushed Bradley, as he knew what Xavier could do to them if he wanted to.

"Take what?" Xavier said, taking a few steps closer to Bradley.

"Sorry, sir," Peter said in a desperate attempt to keep Xavier calm. "Brad's just excited. He didn't mean any disrespect to you."

To their relief, Xavier decided to forget Bradley's cocky comment. "Anyway, kids, I am almost impressed," he said. "Almost. But you still have two more to go. C'mon, this way."

CHAPTER 26

Xavier impatiently led them into a huge, empty chamber. It was by far the largest room they had entered here at the ruins, and was likely used to host big ceremonies and events in ancient times. Xavier was visibly irked by how clever and capable this group of kids had turned out to be. "Like most of your other challenges," he said in a powerful yet monotone voice, "your goal is simple: get over there, to the exit."

"We could've figured out that much by ourselves," Bradley blurted out rudely without thinking.

"Brad!" Peter said quickly, nudging him with his elbow. The last thing they wanted to do right now was irritate Xavier even more. What was Bradley thinking? Peter had just finished apologizing for Bradley's last inappropriate comment, and he doubted this one would be forgiven so easily.

"Oh, so you're all geniuses now?" Xavier asked,

113

refusing to let Bradley's comment go unnoticed. "I suppose I should start getting worried then, right?" He paused, and looked at the other three kids, waiting to see if anyone else had something to add. When he was met with nothing but silence, he continued, "Well, now that Bradley here seems to be finished interrupting me, I will continue. There are six blocks on this table. As you can see, each one is a different shape. On the wall behind you, there are six holes. The six holes match the shape of the six blocks."

"This is just like that game we did as little kids," Neil said excitedly. "Where you put the different shapes through the matching holes in the plastic lid on the box. My mom said I loved that game."

Since the game Neil was referring to was only played by two-year-olds, no one, Peter included, could actually remember how good or bad they were at it. But Peter had heard one story countless times about how Bradley used to play that game.

"We better not let Brad touch the blocks today," Peter said to everyone. "Apparently when he was two, he slammed and smashed the square block into the hole for the triangle until he actually broke the lid."

"Whatever," Bradley mumbled, having also heard the same story many times. "Maybe I was just trying to be original. You know, do things my own way."

"Excuse me, AGAIN!" Xavier announced loudly, angry about being interrupted yet again. "Be quiet and let me finish. Once placed in the matching hole, each block initiates some sort of natural force, like wind, or rain, or something else. You may test all six, one by one, in order to find out exactly what each one causes. After you've tried them all, then you must choose which TWO shapes you will use. Put those two blocks in the holes, and then all four of you have to place one hand on the entrance wall. Then the timer will begin, and you will have exactly twenty seconds to run to the opposite wall. If all four of you touch it in time, you succeed.

"Wait a minute," Bradley said. "You mean, if we choose the wind one and the rain one, then we'd have to run through a wind and rain storm? In only twenty seconds?"

"The next Einstein!" Xavier answered sarcastically. "I will be waiting by the far wall. That way I can start the timer once you've chosen your blocks and are ready to start."

"How many attempts do we get?" Peter asked, just as Xavier was turning to walk across the chamber.

"How many attempts?" Xavier replied without turning back to face them. "Weren't you listening? Only one! But since you are a group of *self-proclaimed* scholars, one attempt should be all you need!"

Peter despised the *you only get one try* type of games. He knew even the easiest games and puzzles often involved making a couple of mistakes and then correcting them.

"Don't worry," Nicola said, hoping to raise everyone's spirits a little. "Let's start testing them out. I'm sure we'll be able to figure out what to do once we've seen all six."

"Let's start with this bad boy," Bradley said while picking up the star-shaped block.

The instant he slid it into the star-shaped hole, the ground started shaking violently. They all lost their balance and fell over.

"Take it out, Brad!" Peter yelled.

It took a good ten seconds for Bradley to get up to pull the block out. The shaking was so intense that standing up had been next to impossible. When he finally pulled it out, they all breathed a sigh of relief.

"We certainly won't be using that one," Neil said. "We'd have to crawl across on our hands and knees, and we'd never make it in time."

"Next they tried the triangle. Right after Neil pushed it in, hundreds of holes opened up on the walls, and torrents of water gushed into the room. Within seconds, the water was up to their knees, and was quickly approaching their waists. It was coming in with such force that it knocked them off their feet again.

Neil did what he could to haphazardly swim back and yank the block out. Once removed, gates opened in the floor and the water quickly drained away.

"This sucks," Neil said while wringing the water from his shirt. "It's like having to choose how you're going to die."

"No one is going to die," Nicola said to reassure Neil. "C'mon, let's try the next one."

They went with the round block next. This one produced an extremely loud high-pitched noise. They all covered their ears in agony. It was impossible for anyone to remove the block, as that would mean exposing a bare eardrum to the piercing noise again.

Before anyone got any permanent hearing damage, Bradley somehow managed to knock the block out with his elbow.

"Well, we can scratch that one off the list, too," Neil announced.

The fourth block, shaped like a diamond, caused a powerful wind. It was so strong that it blew them all back against the entrance wall. It felt like they were glued to it. It reminded Peter of a school trip he'd taken in Grade 7, where his class was allowed into a wind tunnel used for testing airplane wings.

The only way to make any forward progress was to crawl on their hands and knees. But they would never be able to crawl across the giant hall in twenty seconds.

Bradley pulled the block out. Exhausted, all four of them lay on the ground.

"Let's catch our breath before trying the next one," Peter suggested.

A couple of minutes later, they all sat up and leaned against the entrance wall. If the final two blocks were anywhere as severe as the first four, then they were in big trouble.

"Okay, Brad," Peter said once he thought everyone looked ready. "Give the square a shot."

Bradley looked a lot more nervous than he had fifteen minutes earlier. He slowly picked up the square and slid it in. The room started shaking violently again.

"Another earthquake one?" Neil yelled while trying to prevent himself from falling down.

Peter got knocked over right away, and hit his elbow hard when he fell.

"Hurry, Brad! Yank it out!" Nicola yelled, hoping to spare the rest of them from being hurt.

Bradley had an awful time getting up to pull out the block. When he finally got his hand on it, he lost his balance, and smashed his head on the wall. He removed the block while fighting off the pain.

Nicola ran over to check out Bradley's injury. She lightly touched the spot he pointed to, which was already starting to swell up.

"I'm going to have a goose egg here tomorrow,"

Bradley said while testing to see if any blood was coming out.

"I doubt it," Nicola said while giggling. "Your head is pretty thick."

"Very funny," Bradley said with a smile. But Nicola's silly comment had come at just at the right time, as it had prevented Bradley from getting too angry about what had just happened.

Neil picked up the final block, which was shaped like a hexagon. "May I do the honors?" he asked.

"Be my guest," Bradley replied while bowing to him.

Once the hexagon was completely in, the room darkened, and then bolts of lightning shot down randomly in front of them,

"Hey, this one might have some promise," Neil said. "If we just watch carefully to see where the bolts are hitting, maybe we can map out a path across so that they don't strike us."

"Nice idea," Peter said. "But unfortunately, that's not how it works. Lightning always follows the easiest path. If we go out there, it'll use us as conductors. We'd get fried."

"Oh," Neil said sheepishly, "guess I slept through science class one too many times."

Neil removed the hexagon, and they all sat cross-legged facing each other. They had a very big decision to make, and they wanted to ensure that everyone was free to voice their opinions.

But instead of sharing and comparing various ideas, everyone just sat in silence. It looked as if Nicola was getting ready to speak, but she stopped before saying anything. In all likelihood, she had an idea of how to beat *one*. But *two*? There was no chance.

HI READER! (^_^)
WHICH TWO BLOCKS DO YOU THINK THEY SHOULD CHOOSE?

Peter noticed that the rest of his team was now looking his way, like they were waiting for him to make the final decision. The pressure began to make him feel a little uneasy.

"I'm open to suggestions," he said, making eye contact with all three of them while waiting for a response. "Just throw your ideas out there. One might lead to the next."

"Here's mine," Bradley said, catching them a little by surprise. "Wind plus water."

"Wind and water?" Neil asked. "How would that work?"

"You remember when we used to have swim practice at the outdoor pool?" Bradley continued. "When we were swimming, the wind pretty much made no difference."

Bradley had a good point.

"That makes sense," Nicola added. "Plus we are all pretty good swimmers."

Bradley's suggestion did deserve some merit, but Peter needed to run it through the *calculator in his mind* first. He knew that most people swam about four or five times slower than they ran. Gauging the distance they had to cover and the time limit imposed, swimming would be too slow. But he needed to explain this to Bradley in a way that wouldn't sound like he was talking down to him.

"Brad, what's your fastest fifty-meter freestyle time?" he asked.

"Just under twenty-six seconds," Bradley answered proudly. "Third fastest in the entire district."

"Okay," Peter continued. "Well, you know none of us are even close to being as fast as you, right? And we have to get across this whole room, which looks to be about the same length as a 25-meter pool, in twenty seconds. Plus we are wearing clothes, and swimming with backpacks on. You might be able to make it, but the rest of certainly won't."

"Oh," Bradley said, not knowing what else to say.

"I think I might have an idea about how to beat the wind one," Neil said. "One of my cousins is really into cycling, and when they go as a group, they ride in a line to reduce the wind. I think he called it drifting, or maybe drafting, or something like that. If we went across in single file, very close to each other, then only the front person would get the strong wind. We could use our arms to push each other forward. What do you think?"

"If it was only wind, that might work," Bradley said. "But we have to combine it with one more."

Peter started to get a little irritated with himself. This happened quite regularly when he found others were coming up with more ideas than he was. He needed a new perspective. He also wanted to relieve the pressure he was feeling from the rest of his team. He got up and walked a few meters away from everyone, then started pacing around in circles and talking to himself.

Bradley looked like he was about to say something sarcastic to Peter, but Nicola quickly put her hand on his mouth before he had a chance. "Shhh," she whispered to Bradley. "Just let him think. You know that's how he does things."

Bradley then suddenly stood up. It was almost as if a light bulb, indicating that he'd just figured it out, was right above his head. "Believe it or not, I actually remember a couple of things from high school physics," he announced. "And the thing that just popped into my head is this: For each and every action, there is an equal and opposite reaction!"

"Sounds more like poetry than physics," Neil remarked. "And didn't Pete have to help you with all your physics homework?"

Neil was right. Even though Bradley was three

years older than Peter, he was way behind him as far as understanding both math and science. If it hadn't been for Peter's assistance, Bradley never would've passed those subjects in junior high and high school.

"Allow me to demonstrate," Bradley said boldly. "Neil, stand up, face me, put up your hands, and lock fingers with me."

"I don't wanna hold hands with you!" Neil said back quickly.

"Fine," Bradley replied, unimpressed by Neil's reaction. "Pete and Nik, you'll do this, right? Face each other and lock hands."

They quickly stood up and did as instructed.

"Okay, Nik," Bradley continued. "Start pushing Pete backward."

As she pushed, Peter took steps backward to prevent himself from falling.

"Nik, now stop pushing," Bradley said. "Pete, now it's your turn to push."

Nicola began shuffling her feet backward to maintain her balance.

"What's this," Neil asked while laughing, "the waltz of the geeks?"

"Ignore him," Bradley said without even looking Neil's way. "Okay, now I want you to both push at the same time. Ready, set, go."

Being the weakling he was, Peter had no hope of pushing Nicola over. But Nicola wasn't so big or strong either. Neither was losing any ground.

"A dead heat!" Neil laughed. "The wimps are deadlocked!"

"Okay, you can both stop pushing now," Bradley continued, ignoring Neil's remark completely. "Please tell me at least one of you can see where I'm going with this?"

Peter jumped with excitement. "You're a genius!" he yelled. "It's almost too simple, isn't it? Brad, I'm so glad you're here. I totally overlooked this one."

"Overlooked what?" Neil asked, needing to hear the rest of the explanation.

"Don't you see?" Peter said, speaking rapidly because he couldn't contain his excitement. "It's the two earthquake ones we need. I'm willing to bet that if we insert them at exactly the same time, they will cancel each other out!"

"Ladies and gentlemen, it's been a pleasure," Bradley gloated in jest, taking a deep bow in front of his team.

"Are you sure?" Nicola asked.

"99.9 percent," Peter replied. "But that's good enough odds for me. Brad, you take the star. Neil, the square. I'm guessing that one starts shaking to the left, and the other one to the right. If you put them in at exactly the same time, the ground should remain still."

Bradley and Neil got ready.

"On three, guys," Peter said. "One, two, three!"

They slid their blocks in and everyone

immediately got into a stance that would help them remain standing when the shaking started.

But nothing happened. No shaking. Not even the slightest tremor.

"Brad," Nicola said loudly, "you rock! And I always thought you were just the dumb jock."

"Well," Bradley replied, looking a little embarrassed. "I suppose I—"

"C'mon guys, let's win this!" Peter yelled, impatient to complete the challenge. "Line up and put one hand on the wall. Remember, we still gotta run across in twenty seconds or less. And don't do anything stupid, like skip or do cartwheels. If you trip or fall, then you might not make it across in time."

They lined up along the entrance wall, and everyone put one hand on it. On the count of three, they all started sprinting. Getting across to the opposite wall was a breeze. When the slowest of the four, Nicola, touched the wall, only twelve seconds had elapsed.

Xavier pointed toward the exit door without saying a word.

Peter surreptitiously looked at his watch while walking through the door. It was a little past two. They still needed to give Zoltan and Mr. Winchester another hour or so to finish setting everything up...

CHAPTER 27

Xavier led them into the next room, the location for their fifth, and final, challenge. Directly in front of them, there was a steep staircase. At first glance, there looked to be about twenty or twenty-five steps in total, and the riser part of each step had a large yellow *1*, *2*, or *3* on it. The order of the numbers was random.

There were no railings on either side, but they could see the holes where the railing posts had been at some point in the past. Peter's first guess was that Xavier had removed them for today's challenge. Without railings, the staircase looked extremely intimidating. If anyone were to fall over either side while climbing up, especially closer to the top, they'd sustain a serious injury.

Peter knew most staircases were constructed to rise at a thirty-two-degree angle, but this one was clearly not made to follow modern building standards. Instead of the normal thirty-two degrees, this one looked to be closer to forty five.

"Talk about deja vu!" Nicola said. "This reminds me of that checkerboard one we did against Zoltan two years ago."

"No kidding," Neil added. "I remember we had to roll dice for that one, and then—"

"And then," Peter jumped in, "step on only those squares matching the number we rolled."

"Dice?" Bradley asked, not really following the conversation. He had only shown up after they had completed seven of the eight challenges two years ago, so he hadn't seen this checkerboard challenge they were talking about now.

"Well, there's no such thing as a three-sided dice, is there?" Xavier said coldly. He then turned to walk toward the door they had all just come through. "The instructions are simple. At least three of you must get to the top of these stairs." He paused for a few seconds, waiting for any questions. "And don't start whining about the time. You have one full hour, and may make as many attempts as you want."

Peter pressed the button on his wristwatch to start the clock.

Bradley looked at the steps, and started saying the numbers aloud, beginning from the first step. "1, 3, 2, 1, 1, 3, 2, 2, 1, 3, 2, 3, 1, 2," he said. "Pete, maybe there's a code or something hidden in there."

Peter had already begun running the numbers through the *code-cracker* in his mind. He loved number puzzles, no matter the type, and prided himself in being able to crack even the most difficult codes.

"But you guys also see what you can make of it," Peter said. "You've solved just as many puzzles, or even more, than I have today."

Peter wasn't lying about that comment. Although he had the most academic brain, Neil, Nicola, and Bradley provided the creative thinking and ideas that Peter could not.

"For starters," Bradley said. "Why don't I just walk up? I'll go one step at a time, and see what happens."

"Can't hurt," Peter replied nervously, knowing this was just Bradley's impatience speaking. "But don't go too fast."

Bradley started up the steps, going at such a snail's pace that it looked like he was moving in slow motion. Nothing odd or dangerous happened at first, but when he put his foot on the tenth step, which was a *three*, they all heard a loud grinding noise. In less than a second, the steps rotated until they became flush with each other. The stairs had just turned into a flat slide! Gravity quickly pulled Bradley off his feet and he slid down to the floor where he had started. The instant he finished sliding down, the grinding noise occurred again, and the slide rotated back into stairs.

"Wow! That was cool!" Neil said without thinking.

In order to make the amount of pain any one person would suffer after sliding down and crashing to the floor no worse than the other three, they decided to take turns.

"I'll go next," Peter announced. "On the *ones*".

He was doing fine until he stepped on the fifth *one*, which was three steps above the spot that had caused the stairs to rotate for Bradley. The grinding noise began and the exact same thing happened to Peter.

Nicola and Neil ended up suffering the same fate when attempting the *twos* and *threes*, respectively. It appeared that any step beyond the ninth one would cause the stairs to transform into a slide.

"From the tenth step on," Peter said, "every step seems to activate a switch that turns the stairs into a slide."

"What if I climb up to the ninth step," Bradley suggested, "and then jump as far up as I can? I can clear at least five or six. Maybe that's all we need to do. You know, maybe only steps ten through thirteen or fourteen activate the switch."

Although they decided to let Bradley give his idea a shot, Peter had serious doubts about its chances of succeeding.

Bradley leapt high from the ninth step and landed on the fifteenth one. He hoped he was in the clear this time, but just like every other attempt, the stairs changed into a slide again.

"It must have something to do with the order then," Peter commented as Bradley slid down fast and hard.

They took turns trying all sorts of number orders and combinations: going up in numerical order *(1,2,3,1,2,3)*, or reverse numerical order *(3,2,1,3,2,1)*, using *ones* and *threes* only, or *ones* and *twos* only, and anything else they could think of.

But no matter what they tried, their fate was always the same. They could never get past that ninth step. Plus everyone's bottoms were now sore and bruised from the multiple impacts taken from hitting the floor.

Peter looked at his watch. It was ten minutes to three, so Zoltan and Mr. Winchester should be almost finished setting everything up...

"Wait a second," Neil said out of the blue. "I think I might have an idea."

"Sure," Peter replied.

"Maybe someone always has to be standing on one of each of the numbers?" Neil explained. "You know, like there's always gotta be someone on a *one*, a *two*, and a *three*. Since there are four of us, we can easily do this. We move up as a team, making sure all three numbers are always covered. The last person would just have to go ahead and stand on the same number as the second last person. And then we could continue up like that.

"I think I get it," Nicola said. "If we do that, we can move our way up while keeping all three covered."

Peter stood on the first *one*, Neil on the *three*, and Nicola on the *two*. Then Bradley walked past them up to the fourth step, which was a *one*. Step five was also a *one*, so Peter stepped off his *one* and walked up to it.

They carefully proceeded like this, but when Peter got to the tenth step, a *three*, the stairs began to rotate again. They slid down in a big pile and thumped hard on the ground on top of each other.

"Ouch!" Nicola said from the bottom of the pile. Neil's shoulder had accidentally rammed her right in the nose. It was already starting to bleed.

"I'm so sorry. I'm so sorry," Neil apologized, thinking his clumsiness had broken her nose.

"Don't worry," she answered. "I don't think it's broken. Or at least I hope it's not."

Peter had already fished another towel out of his backpack and was trying to stop the bleeding.

Bradley looked down at his watch. "Only seven minutes left guys," he said. "What now?"

When it looked like the bleeding had stopped and Nicola was back up on her feet, they got ready to focus on the task again.

Peter put his hands in his pockets and looked up at the stairs. It was now or never.

"Petey," Bradley said from behind him. "You've got a hole in your jeans, dude. I can see your underwear."

"Yeah," Neil added. "They're purple!"

Peter twisted his head back and spotted the hole. "They're not purple, losers," he said, obviously embarrassed. "They're navy. The color has just faded because they're old. I guess my jeans got caught on something and ripped on the way down."

Nicola tenderly touched her nose a few times. It seemed to be in one piece.

Neil, Bradley, and Nicola noticed the exact moment that Peter got *that look* on his face. He must have just figured something out!

Peter got his team to lean in close, like athletes do in the huddle at football or basketball games.

"Guys, I think I solved it. But you remember what we talked about, right?" he said quietly. "We have to lose this last one. Intentionally. That's always been the plan. That way, Xavier will get the ceremony he wants, which is what Zoltan and Mr. Winchester have been setting up for all day. By now, they should be finished all the preparations."

"Are you sure?" Nicola whispered.

"A hundred and ten percent," Peter whispered back. "Now let's just make a few feeble attempts at the staircase until time runs out."

They tried a few disorganized and haphazard attempts up the stairs, trying to make them look as real as possible. During the final minute or two, Peter did his best to appear to be in outright panic mode. And when the buzzer finally sounded, indicating they had lost, he even forced out some fake tears.

CHAPTER 28

Xavier walked up to them with a sinister grin, like a joker in a horror movie, plastered on his face. He also clapped loudly while approaching them, which was his way of rubbing salt in their wounds.

"Well," Xavier began, "I will admit that you put up quite a fight today. I figured you would get through the first one or two, but never imagined you could solve four."

Peter and his team knew they had to keep the act going. Nicola was forcing out tears and Peter was pacing around in frustration. Neil and Bradley were standing, motionless, staring at the ground in front of them.

"So," Xavier said while rubbing his hands together in excitement, "just like we agreed, you guys now owe me an extravagant welcoming ceremony."

"Yes, sir. We do," Peter replied softly. "Everything has already been set up: the stage, the microphones, the speakers, and everything else. The location is the large hill behind Clearville High School. We chose that spot because with the stage at the bottom and people sitting on the hill, everyone will get a clear view of you."

"You guys certainly seem to know how to do the most important things right, don't you?" Xavier said with a smile. "Shall we all head there now?"

"The ceremony is scheduled to start at four o'clock." Peter replied. "It's about a quarter past three right now, and it'll take us at least twenty minutes to ride our bikes over there. Once we arrive, we'll need a little time to test the electronics and stuff to make sure there are no glitches."

"You really are a precise young man, aren't you?" Xavier said in a mocking tone.

"So we'll start riding our bikes, and see you there just before four. But meet us by the big trees to the right of the stage. That way the audience won't notice you before we make the official announcement."

"I suppose I can handle waiting forty-five minutes," Xavier replied, nodding his head. "Off you go to your bikes, and I will see you there shortly before four. Toodle loo!"

"Pete," Bradley said once Xavier was gone. "You know I drove here, right? I can drive us all to Clearville High."

"Actually," Peter replied, "I knew you drove. But Xavier didn't. I wanted to buy a little more time for Mr. Winchester and Zoltan, just in case they aren't completely finished all the prep yet."

CHAPTER 29

When they rode up to the field it was exactly 3:42, and it looked like at least a few hundred people had already arrived. The hillside was quickly filling up, and more and more people were still pouring in.

They needed to keep up the facade of being upset and defeated, so they hung their heads as they walked toward Mr. Winchester and Zoltan.

Zoltan was holding a handful of colorful pamphlets. It was this flyer, in fact, that had led to the amazing turnout today.

One Day Only! Free Entertainment!
Come and See the Most Amazing Show Ever!
Witness the Best of the Best!
The one. The only – XAVIER!

Show starts at 4pm on September 28.
Be there or be square!

"Pretty impressive ad, don't you think?" Mr. Winchester bragged. "I wrote it in a way that even if Xavier saw one, it wouldn't arouse any suspicion."

Claire, who had been waiting anxiously for Neil to arrive, completely refused to let go of him. It appeared that she planned to continue hugging him until the end of time.

Although Neil was getting a little short of breath from the strength of her hug, he was ecstatic to see her again. "I missed you so much today, babe," Neil said affectionately. "And I am so glad you are now a member of our elite team. Think about it babe, with your help, we are gonna save the world."

Peter was close enough that he caught the last part of that comment, and felt the immediate need to laugh. Before the snicker came out, he quickly walked away. But then after thinking about it a little, he realized what Neil had said was true: They were about to save the world.

Xavier walked up to them just before four o'clock. "It's almost time," he said in an arrogant tone. "Who will be introducing me to my audience of new worshippers?"

"As your servant," Zoltan replied, "that honor will be mine. But we really want to make a bang here, so let me outline the plan for your introduction."

"A little fireworks?" Xavier said with some excitement in his voice. "I like the sound of this."

"Once everyone has found a place to sit," explained Zoltan, "I will warm up the crowd a little. You know, make them really, really, really want to see you. Then when they are screaming for you, I will raise both my arms in the air and loudly announce, 'Allow me to present the powerful, the amazing, the talented, XAVIER!'"

"Not a bad plan so far," Xavier replied smugly.

"Then you arrive from above," Zoltan continued, "in some sort of tornado or something like that. Land yourself beside me on the stage, just behind the second microphone. I taped a yellow *X* on the floor so it will be easy to spot from above."

"Zoltan, you are going to make a wonderful servant," Xavier said, slapping him hard on the back. "I'll be watching and listening for your cue from a place where the audience will be unable to see me."

"Understood, sir," Zoltan replied. "Your entrance is going to be fantastic, and people will be telling their grandchildren and great-grandchildren about it."

Once Xavier had disappeared from sight, Mr. Winchester quietly whispered for everyone to huddle together. "Okay, you all know what to do. Just do everything as planned and practiced. Good luck everyone."

They quickly split up to their respective stations. The time had come to implement the final part of their masterful, yet highly risky plan.

CHAPTER 30

At about ten past four, it looked like everyone, including the last-minute arrivals, had found a place to sit on the hill. Mr. Winchester slowly limped up the stairs to the stage and began to make his way toward one of the microphones. The closer he got to the microphone, the quieter the crowd became.

He cleared his throat a couple of times, and then began loudly, "Ladies and Gentlemen! Children of all ages! I know why you have all come here today. You have come from far and wide to witness something truly magnificent. To see someone more amazing than anyone else in the entire world."

The crowd started to perk up, just as he had anticipated. "But before I introduce the one you are really here to see," he continued, "how about we give Zoltan one last chance to show off his stuff?"

Of course, the audience had no clue who "Zoltan" was, but that didn't seem to matter. They had come for a show, and couldn't wait for it to start. The crowd began cheering. Mr. Winchester, following the advice Peter had given him, began chanting, "ZOLTAN! ZOLTAN! ZOLTAN!" Before he knew it, the whole crowd had joined in.

Zoltan, with his face hidden almost completely by his hood, walked to center stage.

"Bear with me, everyone," Zoltan said into the microphone in a deep voice. "I know you are here to see Xavier. And I really appreciate you giving me this opportunity to be the opening act for such a fantastic show."

Zoltan slowly raised one arm high in the air. That was a cue for Neil, who was hiding high up in a tree at the top of the hill, a fair distance back from the audience. In one hand, Neil was holding a huge bag filled with multicolored confetti.

"The best way to start off any show is with some glitter and sparkle, isn't it?" Zoltan asked the crowd.

Neil opened the bag and emptied its contents. The instant Zoltan spotted the confetti falling, he used his powers to make it spiral high above the entire audience. He guided the confetti to form long, wavy lines, which soon were moving in a pattern similar to the Northern Lights. And finally, he changed the lines into a few big balls, which he sent high up in the sky. The balls exploded like fireworks, and the sparkling confetti twinkled down slowly to the audience.

"My friends," Zoltan said loudly. "Now we are REALLY ready for the show, aren't we?!"

The audience, mesmerized by what they had assumed was some kind of magic trick, ooed and aahed. Claire, who was in charge of the sound system, turned on some mysterious background music to intensify the effect.

With the crowd so pumped up, Mr. Winchester yelled as loud as he could into the microphone, "You think that's impressive? That is nothing, my friends, NOTHING compared to what you will see next!!"

The crowd roared. It was deafening. They couldn't wait a second longer for the main act.

Zoltan cleared his throat and raised both arms high in the air. "Then without any further delay," he announced. "Allow me to present to you the powerful, the amazing, the unbelievably talented... XAVIER!!"

The crowd erupted. They were jumping up and down, begging for Xavier to take the stage as soon as possible.

On cue, Xavier made his spectacular entrance. He had created a long, narrow, transparent tornado, and he was currently spinning inside it. The tornado then moved closer and closer to the stage, and Xavier dropped himself right on the yellow *X*. For added effect, he quickly sucked the massive tornado into the palm of his left hand. Then he slowly looked up and raised his arms in the air.

The already erupting crowd increased the decibel level even higher. Xavier kept his arms raised high, revelling in the moment.

It was at least a full minute before the volume of cheering started to taper off. Once the majority of the crowd had quieted down, Zoltan figured it was time to continue. Mr. Winchester had just walked off the stage and was watching everything from behind a tree.

"You just saw the sudden, dramatic, and magical appearance of Xavier with your own two eyes." Zoltan announced. "Wasn't that something??"

They started cheering and clapping instantly. They had all loved it.

"So what could possibly top such an incredible appearance?" Zoltan asked the eager fans. He paused a few seconds for dramatic effect. "How about an equally, or even more spectacular, vanishing act?!"

The crowd screamed even louder. They desperately wanted this show to go on.

Zoltan leaned over and whispered in Xavier's ear, "Create some fog or smoke, and engulf yourself. When it's thick enough so no one can see you through it, walk off the back of the stage.

Once you're gone, I'll slowly make the smoke dissipate. While I'm doing that, slip through the row of trees and go up the back of the hill. Then casually start walking through the audience from behind the last row. They'll eat it up."

"I think I'm already liking this new fame," Xavier quietly replied. "The more drama, the better."

Xavier then leaned into the microphone and said, "Ladies and Gentlemen..."

The crowd instantly became silent.

"Prepare yourselves to witness something BEYOND spectacular!" Xavier exclaimed.

He looked up to the sky, and spoke softly in a language that no one other than Zoltan was familiar with. He slowly raised his arms until they were at a ninety-degree angle from his body. Then he began slowly waving them around in a fancy and beautiful pattern. At first, a light fog began to appear over the stage. The fog then began to expand and become thicker. It would only take another fifteen or twenty seconds before the fog would completely hide Xavier from the audience.

Zoltan gave the thumbs up sign behind his back. That was the cue for Peter and Bradley to start crawling to the middle of the stage from behind Xavier. As soon as Nicola saw them crawling, she pulled the lever, just as planned. This caused the trap door, which was directly under the yellow *X*, to open under Xavier's feet. Peter and Bradley had just arrived at the edge of the opening as Xavier was falling through the trap door.

Xavier was caught completely off guard. The floor below him disappeared so suddenly and quickly that he didn't know exactly what had just happened. All he could tell was that he had fallen feet first into a large box.

Before Xavier had a chance to do anything, Peter and Bradley closed the lid of the box and locked it. The crowd, of course, couldn't see any of this, as the thick fog was completely blocking their view. Nicola pushed the lever back and the trap door closed flush with the stage. Zoltan waited for some of the fog to start clearing on its own, and then used his powers to get rid of the rest. When the crowd saw that Xavier was gone, they burst into applause. But what they were really waiting for was whatever would happen next. The crowd craned their necks in every direction, trying to see where Xavier would reappear.

Xavier, meanwhile, was trapped in the box. He tried to stand up, but smashed his head on the top while doing so. Next he tried kneeling, but the box was still too low to straighten his back completely.

"They think they've trapped me," he said to himself. "The fools. How could they be so stupid?

The instant I get out, I am going to show Zoltan and those kids what happens to those who defy me!"

Xavier sat cross-legged, raised one hand until it touched the roof of the box, and got ready to speak. The box he was trapped in was pitch black, but he knew the door was directly above him. All he needed to do was conjure up a strong gust of wind to blow the lid open. But for some weird reason, something wasn't working right. The big gust of wind he tried to conjure up didn't materialize.

"What's going on?" he said, with a slight tinge of panic setting in. "Well, I guess I'll just burn a hole through one of the walls instead."

He began chanting something, holding his wrists and fingertips together and straightening both arms as far as possible. But the bolt of lightning that was supposed to build up and then shoot from his hands didn't appear. It was baffling. In exasperation, he started yelling, louder and louder. But he had no clue that they had completely soundproofed the box. No one could hear his screams.

Bradley leaned over to Peter, the two of them now kneeling down just behind the stage. "Petey," he said. "I think it worked. I mean, if he could have busted out, he would have done so already, right?"

"Let's hope you're right," Peter replied nervously. "Keep your fingers crossed that we didn't miss anything."

Back inside the specially designed box, Xavier was now kicking, punching, flailing and screaming. He also tried using any and all of his supernatural powers in an effort to escape. But no matter what he tried, it didn't work. There was no way out for him.

"Zoltan!!" Xavier screamed. "This is all your doing, isn't it!? The moment I get out of here, I will make you regret the day you were born!"

The crowd wouldn't be satisfied until the disappearing trick was complete. Xavier needed to resurface, somewhere far away from where he had vanished mere moments earlier.

Neil, the second tallest of the team, had already put on a replica of the hooded golden cloak that Xavier was wearing. Peter's team had noticed that Xavier always wore the same cloak, so they had purchased some golden fabric, and asked Peter's mom to sew a cloak. (When she asked what the cloak was for, Peter *fibbed* and said he wanted to wear it to make himself stand out at the District Science Fair.) In addition to the cloak, Nicola's friend's older sister, who was training to be a make-up artist, made up Neil's face so he looked much older. The chance of the hood being blown back and revealing Neil's face was very low, but not zero. And they wanted to be prepared for everything.

Neil started walking from the top of the hill toward the back row of the audience. He walked very slowly and purposefully. Once he got close enough to be noticed, murmuring began in the crowd as a few people started looking his way.

"Look, there he is!" said one man.

"How did he get back there?" another asked loudly.

The rest of the crowd quickly turned around to have a look. Once they'd all spotted "Xavier," the roars and claps began to grow and grow. However, if anyone were to approach him and get close enough to his face, they might notice it wasn't Xavier. So it was imperative for Zoltan to assist, which is exactly what he set about to do.

While hiding behind a few trees to the right of the stage, Zoltan conjured up a dust storm, which looked like a short and stubby tornado, right in front of Neil. Neil jumped into this dust storm, and Zoltan used his powers to lift Neil above the crowd and carry him all the way back to the stage.

Neil stood at the microphone, but he didn't say anything. He raised his arms and started spinning them around above his head, giving the impression he was about to create some new type of magic. As he did this, Zoltan started creating a storm. First came the dark clouds. Then a powerful wind. Then intense rain. And finally, hail. As the hail stones grew larger in size, the crowd got both scared and angry.

"Stop it!" someone close to the stage yelled.

"Yeah, there are kids here!" another screamed. "What are you trying to prove?"

The crowd quickly grew more outraged, and more terrified.

"What kind of magic show is this?" a man said while standing up to leave.

Some people covered their heads with their jackets. Others started booing loudly. Mr. Winchester limped as fast as he could to Neil. He whispered something in Neil's ear, and Neil brought his hands down. And at that exact instant, Zoltan stopped the storm.

The storm had stopped, but the crowd's anger certainly had not. Zoltan went up the stairs, ran to center stage, and grabbed a microphone.

"We are so sorry, everyone," he pleaded to the angry crowd. "We are terribly, terribly sorry. I think we must have had, well, some technical difficulties. This last illusion went... umm... well... horribly wrong. This is so embarrassing, but... we will have to, um, end the show now. For your safety, of course."

The heckling escalated even further. A few people near the stage even threw some half-filled soft drink cups and cans towards the stage.

Zoltan quickly ushered Neil off the back of the stage. The last thing they needed now was an angry mob chasing after them. Their whole team ran and jumped into the two rental vans they had prepared as their *getaway vehicles*. The box with Xavier in it was hooked up to one of the two vans. They had built the box on a proper trailer with wheels, and even had an official license plate on the back of it. They'd had it hooked up to the van for the entire show, so they could make their escape without any delay.

They sped away through a series of rarely used back roads, in an attempt to make following them extremely difficult. And since the audience's parking lot was fairly far from the hill, they were quite sure no one would track them down.

CHAPTER 31

After about forty-five minutes of winding through a confusing series of old country roads, they arrived at the plot of land with Mr. Winchester's shed on it. Although the land and shed were officially in the old man's name, they had been used by no one other than Peter and Nicola for the last two years.

"Peter, we followed your instructions to a T when building that box," Zoltan said as he stepped out of the van. "You were right. Inside it, he is completely powerless."

Peter had been very carefully watching Zoltan for the past two years, trying to learn about any weaknesses he might have. He wanted to be prepared if Zoltan ever turned on the people of Earth. Those two years of close observation led him to the conclusion that a weather god's powers can be severely inhibited, or possibly even nullified, by two things: darkness and mirrors. Peter's guess was that the combination of both had the greatest possibility of success. Therefore, all the inside surfaces of Xavier's box were covered in shatter-proof mirrors, and it was sealed to be one hundred percent pitch black.

"Yeah," Peter said. "I just thought about how the strongest of superheroes, you know, the ones you see on TV and the movies or read about in comics, always have some sort of weakness. I figured weather gods might have weaknesses, too."

"Looks like your love for comic books finally paid off!" Nicola said, pulling Peter in for a huge hug. "We did it, Pete!"

"Once again," Bradley announced, "we've proven ourselves invincible!"

They sat around outside as night fell. They ate. They laughed. They told silly stories. This oddball group of Mr. Winchester, Zoltan, Peter, Nicola, Bradley, Neil, and Claire had officially bonded. They were like family now. And no one would ever know how this group of seven had just saved millions, or possibly even billions of lives.

"But what do we do with him now?" Peter asked while pointing at Xavier's box. "I mean, we can't just leave him in there. He'll die of hunger and dehydration."

"That's being taken care of, Peter," Zoltan replied. "The lead weather gods, all twelve of them, will be here at midnight to cart away

Xavier. They'll take him back to our planet inside that box."

"Are you sure you guys can keep him in there?" Neil asked, sounding a little concerned. "I mean, what if he figures out a way to escape?"

"Our planet has both advanced technology and highly skilled engineers," Zoltan replied. "And our experts are already building a big replica of this box to serve as Xavier's prison. Don't worry, he will never be able to escape. I can promise you that."

CHAPTER 32

Three weeks had passed since the successful trapping and banishment of Xavier, and life was more or less back to normal. It was a beautiful sunny Saturday morning at Meeks Park, where Peter, Neil, Nicola, Bradley, and Claire were digging into a box of freshly baked chocolate chip cookies.

"Pete, your mom's cookies rock!" Neil said, stuffing a fifth cookie into his mouth. "I could eat a hundred of these!"

"Dude," Peter replied, "if you tell her that, she'll make a truckload for you."

They all chatted away until the box was empty, pausing occasionally to drink some milk. Not only had Peter brought cookies, but he also came with a small carton of milk and five plastic cups.

"Okay, Mr. Smarty pants, and his clan of geniuses," Claire said after standing up, "give this challenge a shot."

It turned out that Claire was both interested in and very good at puzzles and riddles. She was actually almost as good as Peter himself.

Since Peter and his friends had helped save the world, Zoltan no longer demanded that Peter and Nicola create weekly puzzles for him. But they all seemed to enjoy doing challenges so much that they agreed to keep making new ones for each other from time to time.

Claire, realizing how much fun this could be, made a suggestion: She thought it would be fun to form an unofficial "club," consisting of Peter, Nicola, Neil, Bradley, and herself. Plus Mr. Winchester and Zoltan were welcome to participate whenever they felt like it. She suggested they take turns creating the puzzles. And today, it was her turn to be the puzzle-maker.

Peter, Neil, Nicola and Bradley now were standing next to the river at Meeks Park, in the exact place Claire had instructed them to go. Claire passed Bradley a small cardboard box, and then handed Peter an envelope.

"You don't really think you made something too tough for *us*, do you?" Neil said while laughing.

Claire walked over to Neil and playfully punched him in the arm. "Don't underestimate your girlfriend," she said. "And you can save that big macho attitude of yours until you have actually *solved* the puzzle."

Bradley put the box down and opened up the flaps to see what was inside. Meanwhile, Peter removed the note from the envelope, and looked at its contents.

"Come on, man," Bradley said impatiently, "What does it say?"

Peter smiled at Claire, "Wow, you really have made this hard," he said.

"Just hurry up and read it," Bradley repeated.

"I'd love to, but I can't," Peter replied quickly. "It's written in code. We can't even start the challenge until we decipher the coded message."

"I'll be back in a few hours," Claire said while skipping toward her bike. "I'm gonna go home and get my weekend chores out of the way. It looks like you four will be busy for quite some time."

"Ride carefully, babe!" Neil said back to her.

While Peter was trying to decipher the code, Bradley, Nicola, and Neil walked up to him. Really, really close to him.

"What's going on, guys?" Peter asked, twisting his head back and forth to look at all three.

"Petey," Bradley said, putting his hand on Peter's shoulder. "It's been three weeks since we banished Xavier."

"I know," Peter replied.

"Of course you do," Bradley continued. "But, there's still one thing the three of us don't know."

"Something I know that you guys don't?" Peter asked innocently.

"Okay," Bradley replied. "I'll get right to the point. Remember puzzle number five? The one you said you had figured out the solution to, but we had to intentionally lose? Well, we've asked you a few times to tell us the solution, but you always dance around the question or change the subject."

"Yeah," added Neil. "We are almost starting to think you really didn't solve it at all."

"Either that," added Nicola, "or there is some reason why you won't tell us."

Peter paused and turned away from his friends for a few seconds. The real reason he hadn't told them was that he had been planning to adapt the solution into the puzzle he was scheduled to make next weekend.

Peter felt his anxiety rising quickly, so he chose to set the record straight. "Okay, here it is," he began. "I'll tell you, but as soon as you hear the solution, you are all going to be shocked that you missed it."

"Was it that simple?" asked Bradley.

"Too simple," Peter replied. "The fact that it was so simple was actually what made it so hard."

"Come on, enough mumbo jumbo," Bradley said impatiently. "Just spit it out."

"Remember when you guys spotted that hole in my jeans?" Peter asked them.

"Sure do!" replied Neil. "I also recall seeing your lovely purple underwear through the hole."

"Neil!" Nicola said sharply, putting her hand over Neil's mouth to stop him from saying anymore.

"That hole is what got me on track to solve it," Peter said excitedly. "I knew sliding down a flat surface wouldn't rip a hole, so I looked for something sticking out of the ground. I couldn't find anything at first, but after closer inspection, I spotted six small circular stone tiles. They were flush with the floor and exactly the same colour as the stone used on the floor. All six of them were in a line, less than a millimeter away from the riser part of the first step. That's when it just, like, dawned on me: They couldn't have been part of the original stone floor. So that meant they had to be part of the challenge. The only logical thing I could come up with was that they were buttons."

"Buttons?" asked Nicola.

"You got it. Buttons," continued Peter. "I was so sure that I watched them carefully during the final few minutes, while you guys were making those fake attempts to get up to the top. I noticed that the instant the stairs changed into the slide, all six buttons rose out of the ground, but only very slightly. Maybe by a couple of millimeters. So when Brad was sliding down once, and was getting close to the floor, I stepped on a button. It, along with the other five, went flush with the floor again. And at that instant, the slide shifted back into stairs."

"Oh, man!" Bradley yelled. "You mean that for the first fifty-something minutes, it was our own butts hitting those buttons on the floor that caused the slide to rotate back into stairs?"

"Bingo," Peter answered, smiling.

"So the numbers meant nothing?" Neil asked.

"Yup. Absolutely nothing." Peter answered.

"So that's why he said only three of us needed to reach the top," Nicola added. "Because one person needed to stay at the bottom, keeping their foot on a button. All six buttons rose or fell as if they were one, right? So if one button was held down by someone's foot, then none of them could pop up!"

"I think I get it," Bradley said. "As long as the buttons couldn't pop up, the stairs couldn't rotate, right?"

"Bingo again," Peter replied. "Brilliant trick, wasn't it?" He paused, waiting to see if anyone wanted to comment on the solution they had missed. When no one spoke up right away, he quickly changed the subject. "But enough about that. Let's get going on Claire's puzzle. Any of you think we can solve it before lunch?"

"Dunno," Neil replied. "But we will certainly give it our best shot."

Peter loved this stuff: He was hanging out with his girlfriend, best friend, and brother. A confusing and complex riddle was waiting to be tackled. What could possibly make him any happier?

Thank you for reading *Really Puzzled*. I hope you liked it as much, or even more, than the first book of the series! If you enjoyed this book, I would be extremely grateful if you could leave a review on Amazon or goodreads. Thank you so much!

If you have any comments or questions, please e-mail me anytime (pj@pjnichols.com) - I would love to hear from you. And don't forget to head over to my website (pjnichols.com) and try some of my cool, head-scratching puzzles!

Sincerely,
P.J. Nichols

Acknowledgements

My parents, brothers, wife, and son, who through love, laughs, support, and encouragement, make my life so much fun! And that's really what it's all about, right? They are all rock stars!

Freddy and Nikki, (my two best friends in the entire world) who are always there to share in the happy times and comfort in the tough times. They both will drop whatever they are doing to come and help whenever a friend is in need.

Tricia, whose talent for spotting and correcting all of the inaccuracies in the manuscript was amazing! I can't thank her enough.

The readers, (Yes, that's you!) who inspire me not only to continue writing, but also to challenge myself to be more and more creative with each and every new book I publish. Stay tuned for the next book in the *Puzzled* series!

About the Author

P.J. Nichols, as you may remember, loves games. Really, really loves games. And it was this love for games, combined with the inspiration from his son, that led to the *Puzzled* series.

P.J. doesn't believe in regretting things from the past, but he does wish that he had found his passion for writing back in his twenties (or even his thirties!). The good news is that he will be devoting a good portion of his time to writing plenty more original and entertaining stories for you to enjoy!

And when he's not writing or playing games/sports with his son, he's out and about, talking to anyone who is happy to have a chat with him. P.J. finds people so interesting; he gets great joy in listening to people enthusiastically tell their stories. And if he's lucky, he might even get an idea for one of his future books through one of those conversations!

To find out more about P.J.
(and try some cool puzzles!) visit
pjnichols.com

Made in the USA
Coppell, TX
30 March 2021

52691623R00100